JUST A BUNCH OF FLOWERS

To Carole

with love from

Sheila Adby

SHEILA ADBY

Matador
9 Priory Business Park,
Wistow Road, Kibworth Beauchamp,
Leicestershire. LE8 0RX
Tel: 0116 279 2299
Email: books@troubador.co.uk
Web: www.troubador.co.uk/matador
Twitter: @matadorbooks

ISBN 9781800464469

British Library Cataloguing in Publication Data.
A catalogue record for this book is available from the British Library.

Printed and bound in Great Britain by 4edge Limited
Typeset in 10.5pt Adobe Garamond Pro by Troubador Publishing Ltd, Leicester, UK
Cover Illustration: Richard Howard

Matador is an imprint of Troubador Publishing Ltd

For mum and all my flowery friends

Including you, Carole !!

ONE

'This design was inspired by my trip to Barbados,' Gillian said as she placed another flower into her arrangement.

'Give me strength,' Polly muttered under her breath.

Sarah smiled. Polly was never the most patient person at the best of times and easily irritated but on this occasion she totally agreed with her. What was supposed to be an interesting and enjoyable evening watching Gillian arrange flowers was worse than watching paint dry. Had she known it would be this bad perhaps she would not have turned out for the evening but instead stayed at home and watched her favourite soap.

There was a round of applause and an underlying sigh of relief as Gillian placed the final flower into her design and turned it around so her audience could see it. Granted it was lovely, but whether or not it was worth the wait was debatable.

Polly glanced at her watch. Time was moving on, and knowing that Gillian was less than halfway through her demonstration she was getting agitated.

'We're never going to get our tea break at this rate,' she whispered out of the corner of her mouth. 'I'm dying to try one of Edna's infamous flapjacks.'

The chair she was sitting on suddenly felt like a concrete slab beneath her and she started to fidget. She could feel pins and needles creeping up her leg. That was the problem with the chairs in the church hall, comfort was not a consideration when they were purchased. Fortunately she was sitting at the end of the row, so Polly flicked her leg out to the side in the hope of getting the circulation to return. She proceeded to gently exercise it as discreetly as she could.

Sarah looked at her and laughed. 'Can't take you anywhere!'

Polly smiled, aware that she did look a sight. She looked around the hall. One or two of the ladies in the audience had nodded off to sleep; others were gazing around the room or checking their phones for messages, clearly not focussing on the demonstration. At least Polly wasn't the only person in the room who was bored.

'My next design was inspired by the cruise to the Bahamas that I took with my late husband Robert,' continued Gillian, totally oblivious of how the audience felt.

'Thought her husband was called Henry,' mouthed Polly.

'It was but he died. Robert is hubby number two. Think she might be on to number three by now.' Sarah confirmed.

Polly smirked. 'He probably died from boredom.'

Sarah grinned. 'Actually I think he died of a heart attack.'

'Of course, whilst I have some wonderful memories of my cruise it was also extremely sad as that is when I mysteriously lost Robert,' announced Gillian.

Polly's ears pricked up. 'What? How could she mysteriously lose him?' She glanced at Sarah to see if she knew what Gillian meant.

'No idea,' she shrugged her shoulders.

'What happened to Robert?' Polly blurted out. There was a gasp from some of the audience who clearly knew this was a taboo subject. Edna looked over her shoulder at Polly and glared.

Gillian stopped what she was doing and stood to the side of the stage, a rose held firmly in her hand. The colour had drained from her face. 'My husband suffered a terrible accident and died.'

'How dreadful,' muttered the audience. This certainly didn't answer Polly's question and she wanted to ask for more details, but before she could she noticed a droplet of blood drip from Gillian's hand where she was gripping the thorny stem of the rose so tightly.

Gillian composed herself and rushed to finish her arrangement whilst the room was in an awkward silence. It was nowhere near her usual standard, with flowers placed rather haphazardly; Polly's question had completely unnerved her. No sooner had she finished than Edna got to her feet.

'Thank you Gillian, that's lovely.' She lied, feeling slightly embarrassed by the end result. 'Ladies, let's have a cup of tea,' she said, trying to take the attention away from Gillian although she knew that a can of worms had well and truly been opened.

The room erupted into loud chattering, far louder than at other meetings. Needless to say the topic of conversation was about Gillian, and Polly daring to ask the question. Polly made her way to join the queue for the long-awaited piece of flapjack. She turned to the person behind her. 'I was only curious as to what had happened,' she said defensively.

'I heard that he'd fallen overboard,' volunteered Maggie, who was ahead of her in the queue.

'Really? I thought he'd tripped down a flight of stairs,' chipped in another lady.

'I was told that he'd been murdered,' came a voice from the back of the queue. Everyone turned round to face the direction of this comment.

'Murdered? What do you mean?' asked Polly, her eyes lighting up with excitement at the idea of hearing some scandal.

'Well,' continued Lizzy, 'apparently he wasn't very well on the cruise; very sleepy all the time; that sort of thing. He was last seen on the deck one evening, and then he was gone. His body was never found.'

Several ladies, including Polly, crowded around Lizzy. Suddenly their desire for a cup of tea had become secondary. 'Do you think someone pushed him overboard?' came the question everyone was thinking.

'Well, it's all a bit convenient, isn't it?'

'What do you mean?' asked Polly, eager for a snippet of information.

'I'd heard that he was loaded and she was in line to inherit a stack of money. After all, she rattles around in that huge mansion of hers, doesn't she? Just her and her latest fella who I believe she met on the very cruise where Robert died.'

'No way, that's a bit suspicious,' Polly pondered. There was nothing more delicious than a conspiracy theory to get

Polly's grey cells working, other than a slice of chocolate cake, of course.

Edna glanced over in the direction of the group of people surrounding Lizzy. She felt herself getting slightly agitated as she loved to be in control and have everyone do as they are told. Time was at a premium as Gillian was not the fastest of flower arrangers. They needed to vacate the hall before ten o'clock otherwise Edna would have the caretaker on her back; something she didn't want as the last time they overran she ended up in a terrible argument with him. Edna could see that the queue was going nowhere whilst all this gossip was taking place.

'Ladies, can you stop gossiping and get a move on? You can have this discussion when we've finished,' she said with some authority.

Polly felt like a naughty school girl having been told off. Edna was an incredibly bossy person at the best of times but relished in her role as chairman as, in her eyes, this was her ideal opportunity to perfect these skills that she had gained from being a headmistress for many years.

Polly picked up a piece of flapjack and a cup of tea and returned to her seat. Sarah could sense excitement in Polly's behaviour as she sat down beside her. 'You look like the cat who got the cream.'

Polly smiled. 'You'll never guess what I've just heard.' She excitedly relayed the gossip to Sarah.

Edna put a cup of tea down on the table on the stage where Gillian was doing her demonstration. She was frantically sorting through her boxes of flowers ready for her next design. 'I do hope you weren't upset by Polly's question,' Edna asked, genuinely concerned for Gillian's feelings.

'Not at all,' Gillian lied, clearly feeling rattled by the whole experience and being put on the spot.

'How's Charles?' Edna tried to change the subject.

'Fine,' Gillian replied, trying to hide the fact that he was not fine, in fact far from it. Their relationship was a loveless affair and one that Gillian had regretted. She seemed to make the same mistake over and over again. 'Can we get on?' she asked, irritation in her voice as she was desperate for the evening to be over. She just wanted to get home.

After several attempts of banging on the table to quieten the chitchat Edna finally brought the group to order. Gillian raced through the rest of her designs at supersonic speed which took everyone by surprise.

Polly was unable to concentrate on anything for the rest of the evening while Gillian finished her demonstration. So many questions raced through her head: What had actually happened to Robert? Was it an accident or was he murdered, and how did Edna get her flapjacks to taste so good?

TWO

Polly lay awake. Gazing around the room she could just about make out the patch of damp in the corner of the ceiling.

I must get around to sorting that out, she reminded herself. The black stain was beginning to become a permanent feature in her bedroom but there always seemed to be something more interesting to occupy her time. Decorating and house cleaning were way down on her list of priorities judging by the number of cobwebs that had found permanent residence in the corners of each room. Her mind flitted from one thing to another and she was unable to settle enough to encourage sleep.

Why she had said she would compete in the forthcoming area flower show was anyone's guess. It wasn't as though she had nothing else to do, but the challenge of competing at such a prestigious show and the satisfaction of winning a prize seemed to make all the stress worthwhile. The decision was made easy for her when she heard that Amy was competing. Amy and Polly were rivals and regularly competed against each other. Somehow Amy always seemed to come one place higher than her; something Polly was determined to rectify especially with her latest design which was a gravity-defying creation. The title of the piece was 'Balancing Act' and her design definitely lived up to this. But it was because of this that Polly had started having sleepless nights worrying about it. Had she bitten off more than she could chew on this occasion?

She turned over. The brightness of the alarm clock on her bedside table managed to illuminate the whole room with an eerie red glow. It seemed to shout at her that she was losing valuable sleeping time but her mind went back to her evening at flower club.

'Go to sleep,' came a voice from beside her.

'I'm trying to,' replied Polly, knowing that her long-time partner, Mark, never appreciated being woken up in the middle of the night. 'I can't seem to switch off,' she continued. 'There's so much going round my head at the moment, what with the flower show, and other stuff.'

'Bet you're thinking about the woman you saw tonight – the one who gets through husbands like hot dinners.'

Polly smiled. 'Yes, how do you know that?'

'I know you too well,' replied Mark, sitting up in bed.

'I'm just wondering …'

'I know exactly what you're wondering,' interrupted Mark. 'You and your conspiracy theories. Perhaps it's all straightforward. Perhaps she's just been unlucky.'

'More like her husbands have been,' smirked Polly.

'Well there's nothing you can do about it right now, is there? I've got an early start so I'm going back to sleep. You should too.'

Mark was right. After all perhaps there was a simple explanation.

Gillian arrived home late as it was quite a drive from where she had done her flower demonstration that evening. Usually she unloaded all the boxes from her car when she returned from doing a flower demonstration, but tonight she didn't feel in the mood to.

She could see the lights were on in the lounge. This meant that Charles had either fallen asleep watching the news, something he often did, or he had decided to wait up for her which was quite a rarity. He had little interest in her life and what she did.

As Gillian opened the lounge door she could see Charles slumped in the chair. She looked at him. Why she had fallen for him she really couldn't say, other than she felt she always needed a man in her life. There was something reassuring about having a man about the house, especially such a large house.

Charles had been so charming and attentive when she first met him. He seemed polite, kind and genuinely interested in her. He had been married several years before but that had ended in divorce. He never spoke about it and Gillian never pushed him on the subject. At sixty-five he was the same age as Gillian and it seemed they were a perfect match for each other.

After Robert had died, or at least disappeared so suddenly, Gillian didn't want to live in their huge house alone. Gillian had loved Robert in her own way but as their marriage continued they began to drift apart and Robert became somewhat distrusting of her. He had a son and daughter from a previous marriage. Of course they were grown up now but for some reason they couldn't be happy that their father had met someone he wanted to marry. As Robert's body had never been found his will was put on hold so Gillian couldn't sell the house and move somewhere smaller even if she wanted to. This certainly didn't please Robert's children who had their eyes on their inheritance. They thought Gillian was nothing more than a gold-digger and resented her for marrying their father in the first place. Whether there was any truth in this was hard to say, but before going on that fateful holiday Robert had become slightly wary of Gillian's spending habits, which seemed to have no limits.

Gillian could see Robert in every room and she was spooked by this. She needed someone to distract her from her memories and therefore she invited Charles to move in with her. She had bumped into Charles on the final cruise that she had taken with Robert.

To any outsider it all seemed a bit too convenient meeting Charles at the very time that Robert disappeared but Gillian thought it was fate. Charles was so supportive of her while she was trying to come to terms with what had happened. He was her knight in shining armour, or so she thought, and after a fairly short period of mourning she had decided that Charles was the one for her. Despite their pleas, they weren't allowed to get married as it was impossible to confirm categorically that Robert was dead. Determined to be together, Charles moved in with Gillian. Gillian had always been somewhat prudish and was afraid of what people would think if she 'lived in sin' but Charles was persuasive and they agreed to pretend they were married. Gillian wore a wedding ring and started to be known by his surname, and to the outside world they were a loving couple.

Charles had no home of his own as such and never seemed to have any money but this didn't bother Gillian, or if it did she didn't show it. She was just pleased she had met someone she thought she might be able to love one day.

How wrong could Gillian have been? It seemed that having a ring on her finger, albeit a fake wedding ring, changed Charles's attitude towards her and it wasn't long into their relationship that she saw Charles's true colours. He was lazy, arrogant, and had no interest in Gillian; all he wanted to do was spend her money and have a good time with his friends. Gillian started to wonder if this was why his previous marriage had broken down. She knew she had to get out of this marriage one way or another.

Charles seemed motionless as he was slumped in the chair. For a split second Gillian wondered if he was dead. A sense of relief started to fill her but it was short lived as Charles did a loud snort. She looked at him. How she despised him. She wondered why she had felt relieved to believe that he might be dead. Did she hate him so much that his death would free her from such an unhappy situation? At least if he died she wouldn't have to admit to friends and family that she had made a mistake with getting involved with him in the first place. She continued to ponder this scenario as she headed to bed, leaving him asleep in the chair.

THREE

Amy had been awake for hours when Malcolm finally rallied. She glared at him as he headed into the kitchen. He ignored her, as he always did when he first got up. It always took a while for him to fully wake up. He was very much a night owl, whereas Amy was a morning person.

'Tea?' she asked, reluctantly offering.

'Lovely, thanks,' came the reply.

Amy poured the boiled water into the teapot and put it on the table in front of Malcolm. He was busy helping himself to the cereal that had been placed on the table, along with the milk that was already in a jug. The table was set the same way every day. Nothing ever changed. Amy was very much a creature of habit when it came to certain things. For most people a quick sip from a mug of tea, and a bite of a slice of toast as they headed out the front door to work was all that they could manage for breakfast. But Amy liked to do things properly. She always set the table in the kitchen for breakfast. She always used a teapot. She always served tea in a china tea cup, never a mug. She always liked to have milk in a jug and sugar in a bowl. Nothing was ever going to make her change her way of doing things.

Amy was the sort of person who always felt she was better than anyone else. Despite her difficult childhood she seemed to have been born with a silver spoon in her mouth. She had been spoiled by her parents when she was growing up and always got her own way. Mainly because her father was often away on business and compensated for this with anything she wanted, apart from love. She was the only child and never learned how to share with anyone. She never had any friends at school. Resentment and jealousy caused the other children in her class to give her a wide berth. While her friends went out and enjoyed themselves she would sit alone and study. She soon discovered that no one likes a swot. Especially a swot who is always top of the class.

The day finally came when she could leave school. Her parents were very proud of her as she won the prize for being the best student that year and achieved the highest number of qualifications, which allowed her to get a good place at university. Not having many social skills, she thought that if she went to university she could delay having to fully interact with people in a working environment as she would be able to submerge herself in her studies and keep herself to herself.

It was during her studies that she bumped into Malcolm. They would often meet in the library where they started studying together. She liked Malcolm a lot although at times she thought he was a bit of a nerd. However, this didn't prevent their friendship from blossoming as they seemed to be on the same wavelength. Malcolm was besotted with her and Amy took advantage of his feelings.

They both graduated and Malcolm headed into banking. Amy wasn't too sure what she was going to do. Working in the real world filled her with dread and when Malcolm proposed she jumped at it. By then he was earning a good salary and could support her so she took the opportunity to set up home and raise a family. She loved being a housewife and mother, although her relationship with her two children was strained and they both ended up moving out of the house as soon as they were old enough to. This left Amy with a lot of time on her hands. She felt that she didn't have a purpose in her life and set about trying to fill the gap. By chance she heard about her local flower club which she decided to join. It wasn't long before she was fully engrossed in flower arranging and had discovered a natural talent that had been hidden for many years. She also discovered a secret desire to compete and be the best at everything she did and this was her motivation to enter as many competitions as she could. Coming second wasn't an option as far as she was concerned.

Malcolm had learned to live with Amy's passion, and assisted her whenever he could. Malcolm had taken early retirement which was great news for Amy as this meant that he was around during the day time and could be Amy's chauffeur as she had never learned to drive.

Today she was heading out to collect the stand she had commissioned to be made for her exhibit at the forthcoming area flower show. She had spent weeks designing her stand and was excited that she was at long last going to see the finished result. She had found a blacksmith who had a shop not far from where she lived who could make more or less any stand she needed although he was a bit pricey, but that never seemed to bother Amy.

'Can you hurry up?' she asked Malcolm, starting to get agitated.

'I'm trying to have my breakfast.'

'I can see that. I want to get going.'

'When I'm ready,' he snapped.

Amy walked out of the kitchen. She knew that if she stayed she would end up arguing. Malcolm finished eating his breakfast at his own speed and picked up his car keys.

'Ready when you are,' he announced to Amy. She tutted and rolled her eyes. She didn't bother speaking to him as there was nothing to say.

They sat in silence during the drive to the shop. Malcolm knew that when Amy saw her new stand she wouldn't be able to stop talking on the way home. Why she needed a brand-new stand for every competition was beyond him. She had her own large shed in the garden full of stands, many of which had only ever been used once. Whenever he challenged her about spending so much money on these designs she would answer him, 'you want me to win, don't you?' He wasn't sure how to answer that. Of course he always wanted her to win. If she didn't win he knew life at home would be extremely icy for a few days as Amy was not a good loser, but he couldn't understand why she had to spend so much of his money.

He pulled into the unmade lane that led to the shop, slightly concerned by the number of potholes and flying stones that were flicking out from his tyres. He'd only just bought a new tyre so he didn't want to end up with another puncture. His car was his pride and joy and he spent many a Sunday afternoon washing and polishing it.

No sooner had he stopped the engine than Amy jumped out of the car. She could see her new stand in the yard beside the shop and she was excited by what she saw. 'That's wonderful,' she said as she pulled her purse out of her handbag to pay for it.

Malcolm carefully loaded the stand into the car. As far as he was concerned it didn't look much different from several others that were in Amy's shed but there was no way he dared to comment on this fact. If Amy was happy, so was he.

The drive back home was the opposite of the drive to the shop. As predicted, Amy didn't stop talking for the duration as she was buzzing with excitement.

She had previously ordered some flowers from her local florist wholesaler so she could mock up her design, so they made a slight detour on the way home to pick them up.

Yet more expense, thought Malcolm to himself, but that was perhaps a small price to pay for a free afternoon to do whatever he wanted.

Polly had also commissioned a stand to be made for her design, but hers was done very much on the cheap. She had decided to recycle several of her old stands in order to save some money, and also to placate Mark and not add to the collection of stands and pedestals already in the garage. One of her fellow flower club members, Maggie, had a very talented husband, Stephen. He used to work as a welder until he lost his job, although nowadays he found he had so many orders from flower arrangers to make stands for various shows and competitions that he would be hard pushed to find time to go to work.

Polly's requests were always a challenge for him and used to make him laugh. Most people would turn up with a plan and a list of measurements for him to follow. Polly would turn up with a rough mock-up of what she wanted. This could be made out of a variety of materials. Papier-mâché, chicken wire or bent coat hangers would often be used to help explain the design. Even though he needed a good imagination to interpret her design he somehow managed to get it right every time. However, this latest design of hers was a real challenge. There were a number of complications, least of all the stability of the stand. Stephen thought he could find a way around this but he had had several sleepless nights trying to figure out how he could make such a tall stand less precarious. After all, it wasn't just Polly's reputation at stake in the competition. If he made a stand that collapsed he would lose business from other flower arrangers so he needed to make sure it was stable.

Polly arrived bright and early. 'Couldn't sleep,' she said as she got out of her car and saw Stephen standing in his workshop which was a modified garage to the side of his house.

Stephen smiled. 'Know what you mean! I've had a few sleepless nights too. What do you think?' he asked as he showed Polly the stand.

'That looks great,' she said, pleased with what she saw.

'I've made one or two changes to the original design to make it stable. There's no way this will fall over unless you physically push it.'

Polly pushed it slightly just to test it for her own peace of mind, but was satisfied that it barely moved. 'And you're sure that the weight of the top sphere won't pull it over?'

'No, it'll be fine. This isn't going anywhere,' he reassured her. 'Once you've done your mock-up, if there any problems let me know and I can adjust it.'

Maggie had seen Polly arrive but as she had been banned from going into the garage she remained in the house. Maggie was competing in the same class as Polly so Stephen was keeping both designs top secret. He had been sworn to secrecy by both of them as neither wanted to know what the other one was doing. It wasn't a case of them stealing each other's ideas, but knowing someone else's interpretation had the effect of making the situation more stressful. Doubts would start creeping in if an exhibitor knew what another exhibitor was going to do.

When Maggie thought it was safe she headed towards the garage. 'I've made you both a cup of tea,' she shouted out.

'Thanks, we'll be out in a minute,' came the reply.

Polly soon emerged from the garage, beaming.

'Pleased with it?' asked Maggie.

'It's great. How's your design coming along?'

'OK. Need to do a few more tweaks and it should be ready. I heard that Amy is competing. Hope she's not in our class.'

'I can't stand her,' said Polly, although everyone already knew her views on Amy. 'She always looks at me as though I'm something the cat brought in.'

'Me too.'

Stephen appeared and collected his mug of tea. 'I'll leave you two to chat. Give me your keys and I'll put your stand in your car.'

Polly obliged and followed Maggie into the lounge. 'What did you make of last night?' It was still playing on Polly's mind.

'What, the dreadful flowers or the mystery of the missing husband?' asked Maggie.

'The missing husband, of course.'

'Very odd. I wonder what really happened,' pondered Maggie.

'I doubt anyone knows apart from Gillian. Do you think there's any truth in what Lizzy said?'

'Not sure. She does like to gossip so it's hard to know where she heard this. If anything suspicious had happened I'm sure they would've investigated it.'

'Well, I'm going to have a look on the Internet to see if there's any mention of it. After all, it's not every day that someone vanishes from a cruise,' insisted Polly.

'Bet they've covered it up. I doubt the cruise company would see this as a great advert for their company.'

Polly laughed, 'Yes, hardly a selling point. Come cruise with us into the sunset and never return.'

'Absolutely.'

Polly finished the last mouthful of tea. 'Best be off. I'm going to grab some flowers from that new cheap supermarket on my way home and mockup my design. Can't wait.'

Maggie watched as an excited Polly drove off with her new stand.

'What do you think?'

Mark wasn't too sure how to answer that question. Before him was a half-completed design made up of a selection of dead flowers from the garden, a few fresh flowers that had seen better days that Polly had found in the bargain bucket in the supermarket, and a number of dusty silk flowers that she had found in one of her many boxes in the loft.

Polly looked pleased with herself. 'I think it looks great, or at least it will with the right flowers and colours.'

'Yes, it's lovely,' Mark replied quite half-heartedly.

'Is that it?'

'Well, I'm not sure what you want me to say.'

'You just need a bit of imagination.'

'OK.'

'Imagine these silk flowers are yellow. The dead flowers are various shades of orange and the pink roses are orange mini gerberas.'

'Oh yes, I can see it now,' Mark lied. Mark had an analytical brain, not an artistic one, and had little imagination at the best of times.

Polly knew that he had no idea what she was talking about but she could clearly see the finished design in her head and it was looking perfect as far as she was concerned.

'Well, I think it'll be the best work I've ever done. I have a good feeling about this if it all goes according to plan and there are no hiccups along the way.'

'Do you want me to help you clear it away so that we can have dinner?' interrupted Mark.

Polly was shocked. She looked at him in horror. 'No I'm leaving it set up.'

'But the show isn't for a few weeks.'

'I know.'

'So we're going to have this in our living-room all that time?'

'I need to keep looking at it, certainly for the next week while I get everything clear in my mind. Flower arranging isn't about sticking a few flowers in a vase, it's complicated.'

Mark wasn't impressed but knew that this was an argument he would lose. He'd had to live with a flower arrangement in the lounge before, but nothing on this scale.

How he was going to watch TV around this monstrosity was anyone's guess.

'We can't even see the TV,' he protested.

Polly realised that she had got so carried away with setting it up that this hadn't occurred to her. She appreciated Mark had a point, especially as she wanted it to become part of the furniture while she tweaked the design.

'OK, if we carefully move it over to the corner will that make you happy?'

'Yes,' Mark smiled, pleased that he might be able to watch the football later that evening after all.

'I'll slide it from the bottom and you support the top,' ordered Polly. Mark got into position as Polly knelt down and gently eased the stand a few inches. As she did one of the spheres that was suspended from the top started to swing.

Mark burst out laughing, having nearly been hit on the head by it. 'This thing is lethal. It could cause serious injury.'

Polly looked up and laughed as Mark was dodging the sphere. 'Are you OK?'

'Yes, just concussed,' he exaggerated.

Polly tutted. 'Stop making a fuss.' She could see the funny side of it. 'Your face is a picture.'

Having composed himself Mark supported the sphere. 'Right, let's move it a bit further over.'

They carefully slid the design across the floor into the corner of the room. The position was better so at least they could now see the television, but Polly wouldn't be able to get behind it. That was a small price to pay for having Mark happy. The other slight snag was that one of the spheres hung precariously over the dining-table.

'Never mind "talk to the hand", this is like "talk to the sphere", observed Mark as they sat down to eat dinner and realised that if they wanted to have a conversation they would have to try and dodge this chrysanthemum-laden sphere.

'Just hope there's no greenfly,' remarked Polly.

'Great, just what I need. A bit of extra protein,' said Mark, laughing.

'How's it going, dear?' asked Malcolm. He had enjoyed his afternoon. He had taken his beloved car to the nearby car-wash and treated it to a thorough wash and brush up in order to remove any trace of mud after the trek to the blacksmith's earlier that day.

Amy had a smug smile on her face, clearly pleased with the result. She should, thought Malcolm, well aware of how much this design had already cost and this was just the mock-up. He just hoped that the final design went well and she achieved the result she wanted.

'Don't you think it looks great?' she asked enthusiastically.

He stared at the design. He wasn't too sure what it was supposed to be and was surprised at the number of flowers Amy had managed to cram into the arrangement, which made it look rather top-heavy. But he was no judge and assumed Amy knew what she was talking about.

FOUR

Sarah pulled up in front of Polly's house and sounded the horn. She saw the curtains twitch and in a couple of seconds Polly was locking up the house and heading out to the car.

'Let's get this over with,' commented Polly as she got in. 'I really didn't feel like coming this evening. I hope Edna isn't too upset with me after our last club night. She gave me such a filthy look when I asked about Gillian's husband.'

'Maybe it won't be that bad. Perhaps she's forgotten about it,' replied Sarah, trying to sound optimistic as they headed to the monthly flower club committee meeting, although well aware that Edna was unlikely to let it rest. 'I can't believe how quickly these meetings come round,' she said, changing the subject.

'It just seems that every committee meeting is the same. We never make any progress,' replied Polly, feeling somewhat bored with her predicament.

Sarah and Polly had both volunteered to be on the flower club committee a few years ago. Once on the committee it seemed impossible to leave as no one else wanted to have the job despite them trying to persuade people to take their places.

Traffic was almost non-existent and it didn't take long to get to Edna's house, which was on the 'posh' side of town.

'At least one consolation is that hopefully Edna will have baked us some cakes,' said Polly with a smile, starting to feel a bit more optimistic.

'You and your cakes. You're not difficult to please are you?' Sarah laughed.

'No, I don't ask for much in life,' replied Polly as she got out of the car and Sarah locked up.

The front door to the porch was slightly ajar and they could make out the silhouette of Edna through the glass panel. 'Come in,' called out Edna in a shrill voice.

Sarah and Polly entered the house. Edna's house was grand, the sort of house Polly aspired to living in one day rather than the tiny two-up two-down that she shared with Mark. The house had original wooden floors that no one was allowed to step on in their shoes. A line of shoes greeted the visitor in the porch as they were asked to remove all footwear before entering the hallway. Sarah and Polly obliged and headed towards the dining-room. As Polly was walking over the highly-polished floor she looked down at her feet and wished she had checked her socks before coming out. A large hole in one of them allowed her big toe to stick out. She tried to adjust her sock to hide the hole.

Sarah saw her. 'Don't worry about it. No one will see it when you're sitting down,' she said, trying to reassure her.

Polly wasn't convinced. After all, it wasn't as though Polly wore discreet socks. She believed that socks were an item of clothing that should express your true personality and Polly's socks were always the talk of friends due to their brightness and outrageous designs. Today she was wearing red and black striped socks with a ladybird pattern and sadly, a toe sticking out the end of them didn't blend well with the design, especially as Polly had only just had her toenails painted bright blue.

Polly and Sarah stepped into the dining-room where the meeting would take place. Barbara was sitting at the table next to Julia. Both were totally engrossed in discussing their recent WI trip to Southend. Edna was flitting about in her usual queen bee manner and Lizzy and April were gazing out of the conservatory window into Edna's garden and discussing the variety of flowers growing there. Edna and her husband, George, were great gardeners and their perfect garden put most other peoples' gardens to shame. George had been a Colonel in the army, and with Edna's need to control pretty much everything, their garden was quite regimented and immaculate – not a blade of grass out of place.

Edna walked into the dining-room and sat down. 'I like your nail polish,' she commented when she saw Polly's toe sticking out prominently, although with the blue nail polish you would have to be blind to miss it.

'Trust her to notice,' Polly whispered to Sarah, feeling slightly embarrassed.

'Ladies, can we make a start?' Edna said somewhat formally but totally in character. The others sat down at the table and noticed a few empty seats.

'Where are the others?' questioned Lizzy.

'Hilary and Freda are on holiday, and Rose is sick,' replied Barbara as she read from her notebook. As club secretary she took her role very seriously, especially as having Edna as chairman was not the easiest of people to work with. They had known each other for years and Edna had been very supportive when Barbara's husband died suddenly. It was Edna who introduced Barbara to flower arranging at that time and it became a lifeline for her. She put her heart and soul into this hobby that now seemed to dominate her life.

'So is everyone happy with the minutes from the last meeting?' quizzed Edna. 'Am I OK to sign them?'

Polly didn't want to admit that she hadn't actually got around to reading them but she was sure they were correct, and even if they weren't any comments she had were unlikely to be taken seriously.

'There are a couple of points,' remarked Julia as usual. 'I know they are both Scottish but it is Lorna who is down to have the tea party next month, not Morag, and you've spelt Katherine's name incorrectly. She's spelt with a K not a C.'

Polly rolled her eyes. She knew that Barbara didn't appreciate having her minutes corrected, especially having typos pointed out to her. Trying to minute the meetings was considerably challenging at the best of times with the conversation jumping from one subject to another and everyone going off at a tangent.

Barbara reluctantly scribbled down the corrections on her original pristine copy of the minutes and handed them to Edna to sign before anyone else could make any more changes.

'Are we all set for the workshop for the next club night?' enquired Edna.

'How many pints of milk do you think I should buy?' came the usual question raised by Barbara at pretty much every meeting when a workshop was being arranged.

'Two pints will suffice. Have you got enough tea, coffee and sugar?' queried Edna.

Polly switched off from the conversation. She'd heard it all before and was beginning to lose the will to live.

'On the subject of the cake rota,' not that anyone had mentioned it but it was clearly on Edna's mind, 'I'm baking the cakes again for the next meeting.' Edna made out that she was annoyed to have this task land in her lap again, but in reality she enjoyed having to be relied on.

Edna moved on to the next subject on the agenda. 'Fundraising,' she announced. 'Anything to report?' There was silence round the table.

'Has anyone got any ideas?' she enquired but was greeted with blank faces. 'In that case we'll defer this until the next meeting.' This was something that happened at every meeting.

'Wait a second,' interrupted April. 'Isn't Rose organising a stand or something at the supermarket for us to raise money?'

'Oh yes. I remember now. Well, as she's not here we'll discuss this next month,' acknowledged Edna. 'How's the coach trip to Winchester flower show coming along?'

'Everything's under control. I've still got a few more seats left on the coach but it should be fine. No more single rooms are available at the hotel though,' answered April, who was in charge of booking these trips. 'I'm surprised at how many people don't want to share.'

'I don't like sharing. I snore and go sleep-walking so no one ever wants to share a room with me,' said Lizzy, laughing.

'Doesn't it worry you that you might sleep walk out of your room?' Sarah was curious.

'When I'm away from home I always put my suitcase on the floor up against the door. That way if I do go sleep-walking, hopefully I'll wake myself up.' Lizzy paused for a second before continuing. 'Although the weird thing with sleep-walking is that you manage to walk around objects, so there's no guarantee this will work.'

'I hope you don't sleep in the nuddie, then,' commented Polly. 'Could be a bit embarrassing if you wake up in the corridor or hotel lobby stark naked.' The thought of it made her laugh.

'What about your husband? How does he put up with you?' enquired Julia, curious as to the sleeping arrangements.

'He's as bad as me. He snores so loudly he can't hear me snoring,' replied Lizzy

'Can we get on?' snapped Barbara as she tried to bring the meeting back to order. Once again the committee had gone off on a complete tangent.

Edna looked at the agenda. 'Treasurer's report. Hilary has sent this in as she couldn't get here this month.' She pulled out a piece of paper that Hilary had given her with the latest figures written on it. 'Club funds are looking quite healthy at the moment,' she observed, pleased to see such a large bank balance.

'Don't forget that a lot of the money for the coach trip is in the bank account,' interrupted April, afraid that the money earmarked for the outing to Winchester might get swallowed up into the club funds.

'Oh yes. Well, even taking that into consideration the funds are still quite good.' Edna realised that Hilary had failed to itemise the trip on the piece of paper and in all honesty Edna wasn't totally sure what she was looking at.

'Why don't we automate our accounts? Surely it would be easier to have this on a spreadsheet,' suggested Polly.

'This way of doing things has worked extremely well for the last twenty years, why on earth would we want to change anything?' asked Julia, genuinely confused by Polly's question.

'It's about bringing the club into the twenty-first century. No one keeps books this way any more do they?'

'Well, we do and nothing is going to change that.' Julia defended Hilary's way of doing things.

'We're not going to discuss this now. Hilary does a fantastic job and there is no reason to change,' although Edna just assumed this as she was not numerate by any stretch of the imagination and trusted that Hilary knew what she was doing. 'Next item; our last club night.' Edna dismissed Polly's suggestion rather rudely and hurried the meeting along, much to Polly's disgust. 'What did everyone think about Gillian? Any good or bad feedback from our members?'

'I think most people liked her, it was just that she was incredibly slow,' noted Barbara.

'Well, only during the first half,' recounted April.

'The second half she raced through so quickly no one had much of a chance to see what was going on,' observed Lizzy, well aware of the reason for the sudden change in speed.

Polly looked at her and then at Edna. Edna was gazing at Polly over the top of the gold-rimmed glasses that were perched on the end of her nose.

'I'm sorry if I said the wrong thing,' stuttered Polly. 'I didn't realise there was a problem about her husbands.'

'I thought everyone knew that discussing Robert's disappearance was a taboo subject.'

'Well, obviously not,' replied Polly. 'I've never heard about him and certainly not about the circumstances of his death. Had I known it was going to cause a problem I would never have mentioned it.' Although this wasn't strictly true as Polly was always fascinated by stories like this.

'No one knows the circumstances for sure,' chipped in Lizzy.

'I wish you wouldn't spread idle gossip, Lizzy,' commented Edna.

'I'm not. I'm just saying that the circumstances were odd. How come they didn't find a body?'

'If he fell overboard in the night there's no way they would've found him. By the time they'd realised he wasn't there it would've been impossible to track him down,' pointed out Edna, convinced that nothing untoward had happened.

'Maybe he didn't fall overboard. Maybe he was pushed or he faked his own death in some way or another,' surmised Lizzy, remembering the rumours she'd heard about him being murdered.

'Now you're sounding ridiculous. Who would want to push him overboard and what on earth would be gained in faking his own death?' asked Edna.

'I'm not being ridiculous and I resent you for saying that. I'm only saying that no one knows the answer so anything could've happened.'

'We shouldn't waste any more time on this subject, speculating what might or might not have happened,' snapped Edna. She glared across the table. 'These meetings aren't for us to gossip about people, there are far more important things for us to discuss. I'm going to put the kettle on and get us all some cake.'

It didn't take much to annoy Edna. Whenever she felt she had lost control she seemed to react, but the mention of cake caught Polly's attention. She pulled a face at Lizzy, which made her laugh. Everyone sat in silence for a few minutes while Edna made the tea.

'Shall we go and help her?' asked Julia, breaking the silence and concerned that Edna was clearly annoyed with them.

'Leave her to it,' suggested Barbara, who had experienced Edna's behaviour for years and knew that on an occasion like this it was best to give her a wide berth.

After some clattering in the kitchen, Edna returned a short time later with a tray of her best china and a delicious looking chocolate cake.

'That looks fantastic,' commented Polly, trying to calm Edna down as she placed the tray on the table in front of her.

'It's a recipe Margery gave me. She calls it her happy cake,' Edna informed them. She was definitely looking calmer now.

'Interesting name. Then again, let's face it, chocolate makes most people happy,' observed April, who was clearly on the same wavelength as Polly.

Edna proceeded to cut generous portions of the cake.

Polly grabbed hold of the teapot. 'Mind if I pour mine now before it gets too strong?' She liked the colour of her tea to resemble dishwater. Anything stronger than that made her cringe.

'How on earth can you drink tea that colour?' enquired Lizzy.

'Easy. The art is to make sure that you can still see the bottom of the cup. Anything more than that and it's too strong.'

'I couldn't drink mine like that,' volunteered Barbara. 'I like builder's tea. Strong enough to stand a spoon up in it.'

'Well, I used to. That is until everyone kept leaving the milk out of the fridge in the office where I used to work. I decided not to risk having milk in my tea after having a jippy tummy one day. I'm sure the milk was on the turn,' confessed Polly.

April ignored the exchange of niceties and continued to rummage in her handbag for her own herbal teabag to dunk in the cup of hot water that Edna had placed in front of her.

'This cake is delicious,' commented Lizzy as she took a large bite of the slice on her plate, not waiting for Edna to hand her the pastry fork. 'I'd love this recipe. How do you get it to taste so chocolatey?'

'The secret is to dissolve the cocoa in a little hot water before adding it to the cake batter,' replied Edna, pleased to be given the opportunity to brag at her baking knowledge. 'Plus there's a secret ingredient,' she continued.

'What's that?'

'I can't tell you, I'm afraid. Margery gave me a bag of dried herbs to add to the mix. No idea what was in it.'

'Funny how lots of cake recipes now contain herbs. I made a lovely banana and thyme cake the other day. Absolutely delicious,' announced Polly. 'Does Margery still practice herbalism?'

'I'm not sure I'd consult her. She's a lovely lady but, not being rude, she's a bit dippy. I'd worry that she'd give me the wrong herbs,' confessed April.

'What, go to her for a headache and end up being treated for something completely different?' asked Polly quite innocently.

Barbara started giggling. It wasn't often that she laughed but when she did it was quite infectious. 'I'd heard that Lorna's husband went to see Margery for a treatment for athlete's foot and Margery ended up giving him the equivalent of Viagra.'

'I bet Lorna wasn't expecting that!' sniggered Sarah.

Edna tried to stifle her laughter as she did not want to appear as though she approved of what was being said, but somehow it managed to find a way out and she burst out laughing. 'You're so naughty,' she said, in between laughing. 'We shouldn't be gossiping like this.' Lorna was incredibly stuck up and her husband totally hen pecked and the idea of her husband being overly amorous amused her.

'What about Amy?' Sarah ignored Edna.

'Skinny bitch.'

'Excuse me?' Edna was surprised at Polly's comment.

'Well she is. She's lost so much weight. She looks like a shrivelled-up prune with stick legs.' It was common knowledge that there was no love between Polly and Amy.

'She does look very gaunt these days,' agreed Sarah.

'Perhaps she fancies herself as a size zero model. What with all her fancy designer clothes she looks like mutton dressed as lamb. I'm amazed her husband can afford to live with her.' Lizzy made her feelings known. She had been at the sharp end of Amy's tongue before now.

'Did you know that she takes photos of everything she's going to eat each day and posts the photo on a social media site?' added Sarah.

'I'm surprised she can operate a computer, let alone be computer literate,' commented Polly in quite a catty way.

'It's some new diet fad thing. They confirm what you can and can't eat,' continued Sarah. 'How weird is that?'

'Well, if I sent photos of my dinner to someone each day they'd think I ate roadkill,' stated Julia.

Tears rolled down Barbara's cheeks as she remembered a particular meal she had eaten at Julia's. Everyone knew that Julia didn't possess the greatest culinary skills. Anything she baked rarely resembled what it was supposed to and to this day Barbara still had no idea what it was she had eaten on that one particular occasion.

'No one tells me what I can and can't eat,' remarked Polly, well aware she could easily shed a few pounds or even stones without anyone noticing.

'Unless of course they say that you can eat cakes, sweets or crisps,' remarked Sarah.

'That sounds like my kind of diet,' confessed Lizzy.

'Me too,' agreed April. 'Life is too short to go without cake. Especially a cake as tasty as this one.'

The laughter continued while the ladies finished their tea, and they all came back for second helpings of the chocolate cake until there were just a few crumbs left on the plate.

George, Edna's husband, warily opened the front door, well aware that usually all he could hear on a committee night was heated discussions bordering on arguments. He was surprised to hear the sound of laughter coming from the dining-room.

'Everything all right, ladies?' he enquired as he put his head round the door. 'You sound like you're having fun this evening.'

Edna looked at her watch. 'Goodness, is that the time?' she said, unaware of where the evening had gone. 'If there's nothing else to discuss I suggest we end and I'll see you all at the workshop at club next week.'

It took a while for the ladies to gather up their belongings as they were all still laughing. Edna wasn't too bothered. For once everyone left the meeting still speaking to each other, which was quite a rarity. After some time they headed out to their cars parked outside Edna's house. Edna could still hear them laughing as she closed the front door.

FIVE

Margery arrived at the hall slightly late. The committee were all rushing around in their usual fashion, setting up the hall and putting the chairs out for the evening's event.

'Bring those chairs over here,' barked Edna in her typical authoritarian manner.

Lizzy and April obliged although resenting being spoken to in this way.

They began setting up half-a-dozen tables ready for the evening's workshop.

'I don't think we need to put too many tables out. We'll be lucky if we get a couple of dozen members turn up this evening,' commented Lizzy. Workshops never attracted many members for some reason.

The tables were extremely old and quite dangerous to assemble as it was easy to catch a finger or two in the mechanism. Lizzy laid the table on its back on the floor and proceeded to force the leg mechanism with her foot. Once the legs of the table were in position Lizzy and April stood the table the right way up.

Hilary, now back from her holiday and sporting a suntan, settled down at a table in the entrance to the hallway ready to collect the entrance fees from the members. Julia sat with her in the hope of persuading members to purchase raffle tickets. Although this evening the raffle prizes were nothing to get excited about so she knew she had her work cut out for her. Apart from a plant that Edna had bought as a prize everything else had been donated by committee members, which consisted of some toiletries, a bottle of wine and a box of chocolates very close to the sell-by date. It wasn't long before the members started to arrive.

Edna was still busy setting up the cake table, trying to make it look appealing. After the success of her 'happy cake' at the committee meeting a week earlier she decided to bake another one. It took pride of place in the centre of the table, surrounded by a selection of highly-decorated fairy cakes and rather bright floral serviettes.

Polly would usually play hostess to the demonstrator and run around after them; unloading their car, setting up their equipment and making them tea. But tonight as there was no demonstrator she had some free time on her hands. She walked across the hall to where Margery was organising her plant sale to see if there was anything that caught her attention. She was always tempted by plant sales and, despite having a tiny garden that was already crammed full of plants, she could never resist trying to fit one or two more in. She glanced at the variety of plants that Margery had brought with her and her eyes settled on a particular group of flowerpots that she found intriguing.

She turned round to face the direction of Sarah who was still helping Lizzy and April set up the tables. Having caught Sarah's eye she started to beam and signalled towards Margery's plants.

'What?' mouthed Sarah from across the room. She knew that something was funny but couldn't work out what exactly.

Polly smiled and headed over to speak to Edna.

'Edna, have you got a minute?'

'Can it wait?'

'Not really.'

'What's the matter?'

'When Margery said that she wanted to bring some of her pot plants to sell, what do you think she meant?'

Edna looked confused and frowned. 'Some of the plants she'd grown.'

'Well, I can confirm that she definitely brought some pot plants with her.' Polly tried not to laugh.

Edna had no idea what Polly meant and she looked blankly at her.

'Unless I'm mistaken, some of the plants she is selling,' Polly looked around her to check no one was listening, then whispered to Edna, 'are cannabis.'

Edna's face flushed. 'What?'

'You heard me correctly.'

Edna glanced over in the direction of Margery's table. Several members were examining the plants.

'That would look lovely in a flower arrangement,' commented a member who was fingering the leaves on one of the cannabis plants, unaware of what variety it was.

Polly could not contain her laughter any more. Sarah headed over to find out what the commotion was all about. They stood and watched Edna as she sidled up to Margery.

'Margery, I've noticed you selling pot plants on your table.'

'That's right. Lovely aren't they, and so versatile.'

'I had no idea you were going to turn up with cannabis plants,' she said quietly, afraid that someone would hear.

'Well, yes, but a little bit of that never did anyone any harm,' insisted Margery, refusing to see the bigger picture. 'And they have such beautiful leaves.'

'They're illegal – you could get us into serious trouble if anyone found out. Remove them from this table immediately,' Edna ordered.

'You didn't complain when I gave you some dried leaves the other day,' Margery protested.

A worried look appeared on Edna's face as the penny started to drop.

'You mean that bag of mixed herbs? The ones that you said needed to be added to the chocolate cake recipe you'd given me?'

'Of course. I said it was my happy cake recipe.'

'I thought you meant that it made people happy because of all the chocolate. What have I done?'

'Didn't you like the cake?'

'Yes, I did. But there's no way I'd have given it to anyone had I known what the ingredients were.' Now Edna understood why the tone of the committee meeting had changed. She thought that everyone had decided to put aside their differences for once. She didn't realise that her cake had got everyone stoned. How she would ever live this down if people found out was hard to imagine.

Polly could see Edna looked embarrassed as she headed back in her direction.

'Is that what the secret ingredient was in our cake the other evening?' Polly teased.

Edna thought about lying to her but knew that Polly had clearly sussed out the situation. 'It would appear so,' she said, extremely tight-lipped.

Polly smiled. 'If it's any consolation that was the best committee meeting we've had. Perhaps we need that at every meeting.'

'I don't think so.' Edna tried to compose herself, but let a slight smile appear on her face. She suddenly remembered the chocolate cake that she had placed on the cake table.

'Polly, can you get rid of that cake?' She pointed. 'I'll quickly pop to the shops and buy a few more cakes, but there's no way I'm allowing our members to eat that.'

'What do you want me to do with it?'

'Whatever you like. Just make sure it isn't here when I get back,' she said as she grabbed her coat and handbag and rushed out of the hall.

Sarah noticed Polly removing the cake. 'What are you doing with that?'

'Edna told me to get rid of it. It would appear that the secret ingredient is pot!'

Sarah laughed. 'You said that Mark thought you were either stoned or drunk the other night when you got in from committee. How right he was.'

'Yes, he'll laugh at this. He said it was the first time I'd ever come home from a committee meeting laughing instead of ranting or crying!'

Polly found a bag to put the cake in and put it in her car. She wasn't too sure what she was going to do with it – whether to throw it away like Edna had instructed, or perhaps take it home to eat later. After all, she didn't want to waste such a tasty cake.

By the time Edna arrived back at the hall with her shop-bought cakes a number of members had already set themselves up on the tables ready to start the workshop. Julia had agreed to run the workshop on this occasion and had positioned herself at a table at the front of the room ready to begin.

'Would you like to start, Julia?' Edna called out on her way to the kitchen, grabbing the cake plate on her way. She quickly unwrapped the purchased items without anyone seeing. Whilst it was fairly obvious they were shop-bought she didn't want to make a big issue of the fact.

When she returned to the hall Julia was in full flow trying to explain the complexity of making a wire handbag before filling it with floral foam and flowers.

'Everything under control?' asked Polly.

'I think we might have got away with it,' confirmed Edna. She glanced over to where Margery had her plant sale and was surprised that Margery had already packed up and was in the process of loading up her car.

'Why are you leaving so early?' asked Rose, concerned that some of the members might have wanted to purchase plants.

'I know when I'm not wanted,' she replied, clearly put out by Edna's behaviour earlier in the evening. 'Edna knows why.'

Before Rose could ask any more questions Margery had left. She glanced over to where Edna was and noticed that she was deeply involved in a discussion with one of the members so she decided not to bother her.

Polly walked around the room helping the members with their designs. She stopped to chat to Maggie.

'How did the mock up go?' Maggie was curious.

'It was great. I'm so pleased with the stand. Mind you Mark isn't very happy with it set up in the living-room.'

'That doesn't surprise me. Stephen hates it too when I'm mocking up, but that's one of the consequences of competing in these shows.'

'I think Mark will be pleased when I get rid of it. Must admit that I don't blame him on this occasion. Part of it is overhanging the dining-table, and the flowers are starting to go a bit manky now.' Polly laughed.

She looked at the handbag that Maggie was making. As expected, it was exquisite. Maggie definitely had a natural talent for flower arranging and anything craft-based.

'Best help Edna with the tea,' she said as she headed into the kitchen to boil the kettle. The members helped themselves to cakes, although some were surprised by the selection available that evening. Edna didn't admit to buying some of the cakes and tried to push her home-baked fairy cakes instead.

By the time the evening drew to a close all the members were happy with their designs, although some weren't as happy with their raffle prizes.

As soon as all the chairs and tables were cleared away, Polly made a quick exit before Edna could ask her what she had done with the chocolate cake. Her mouth watered as she drove home as fast as she could with the happy cake sitting in the boot of her car.

SIX

Margery was up with the lark as usual. As she got older she seemed to need less and less sleep, although she'd always survived on a fraction of the amount of sleep most people needed. She looked at the box of plants she had brought back with her from flower club. She had sold a lot during the evening, which would have been considerably more had Edna not become so prudish and banned her from selling her beloved pot plants.

Margery couldn't understand Edna's attitude. As far as Margery was concerned plants are plants and if they have medicinal properties then they are extremely valuable, no matter what the law said.

Margery had never been particularly interested in herbal medicine or anything complementary, until she met Duncan, that is. It was as though he was having an affair with the world of herbs. He saw plants in his own unique way. Plants all had a reason for existing and if man learned to live in harmony with them his life would be enhanced.

In all honesty Margery thought Duncan was a bit mad

initially until she got bitten by the bug. In the early days of their relationship she would often mock him for talking to his plants, saying that he was crazy, but as they headed deeper along their path together she realised there was a lot of truth in what Duncan said. She started to see plants in a totally different light and she tried her best to learn as much as she could about Duncan's passion.

The slight snag was that Margery appeared to suffer from a form of dyslexia when it came to plants. She had never been the brightest of people and remembering plant names and the finer details was not her forte. She either got the names mixed up or mistook one plant for another, with potentially serious consequences.

'Does it matter that much?' she asked Duncan innocently one day when he discovered that she had given her friend a bag of herbs to treat constipation.

'Those herbs treat diarrhoea,' he informed her.

'Oh dear. She's not going to be very happy with that.' Margery laughed, not understanding the full implications.

'You must be careful. After all, you're not qualified so if you give the wrong herbs you could get into serious trouble,' stressed Duncan, worried that Margery might make a fatal mistake at some point.

Life moved on and Margery and Duncan were extremely happy together. Then came the devastating news that neither of them wanted to hear; Duncan had cancer. He made the decision to treat it himself and turned his back on chemotherapy. For a while everything was fine but gradually he deteriorated and the pain got worse. It was during this time that he started to grow cannabis plants. He had heard of people using this to control pain and felt that, providing he was only using it for his own health reasons, he wasn't doing anything wrong. For the next couple of years he grew these plants and treated himself with their medicinal properties but after a long fight sadly the cancer won.

Margery's life was thrown into turmoil. She had lost her soulmate and felt very alone. During this time she closed the door on Duncan's life as a herbalist, but then realised that this was her way of keeping his memory alive. She decided to continue in his work and set about growing the various herbs, drying them and prescribing them as he had done, or at least more or less the way he used to.

Edna was still seething at Margery's behaviour. 'How dare she turn up with cannabis plants,' she snapped at George, who was quietly eating his breakfast whilst doing the crossword puzzle.

He looked up from the newspaper. 'Perhaps it's an innocent mistake.'

'There was nothing innocent about it. She knew exactly what she was doing.'

'Maybe she just doesn't understand the law.'

'Well, I certainly pointed that out to her. I can't believe the position she has put me in. I could go to prison for this,' said Edna, blowing it all out of proportion.

'I don't think so.' George tried to reassure her but Edna had gone off on one of her rants.

'After all, what would people think of me? How will I live this down? That I drug my visitors.'

George had learned over the years that when Edna was in this state he was unable to reach her and had to wait for her to calm down in her own time. He sat quietly, watching her, waiting patiently until she had reached a place of reason.

'Do you think she just grows the odd plant or do you think she's set up to grow them commercially?' he asked when he thought it was safe to do so.

'What? Like the people down the road?'

Edna recalled the case she'd read recently in the local newspaper of some tenants growing hundreds of cannabis plants in their rented flat. It had been going on for ages but the constant glow of light day and night, and eventually the smell, had alerted neighbours to the problem. When the police arrived they couldn't believe the haul of plants they confiscated.

Edna wondered if Margery was operating on this scale. She doubted it, but there was only one way to find out. She would have to pay her a visit.

Margery wasn't expecting any visitors and especially not Edna. She looked surprised to see her standing on her doorstep. Perhaps she's come to apologise, she thought unrealistically. Edna wasn't known to be the sort of person to apologise to anyone. She always seemed to have an excuse for her behaviour or was totally unaware of how it affected some people.

'Hello,' Margery said to her, reluctant to allow her into the house.

'I wondered if you had a minute. Can I come in?' Before Margery could answer Edna was pushing past her into her hallway.

'Come into the kitchen,' offered Margery, knowing she couldn't turn Edna away. 'I was just about to have a cup of tea. Would you like one?'

Edna was slightly concerned Margery might have her own concoction of tea but was relieved to see some standard teabags on the kitchen table. 'Yes please,' she said as she sat down. 'I'm sorry if I was a bit off with you last night,' she stuttered, trying to get the words out as apologising didn't come naturally.

Margery was taken aback by surprise.

'I just wasn't expecting you to turn up with *those plants*,' continued Edna.

Margery didn't respond. She knew Edna was about to launch into a full-blown lecture and she wasn't disappointed.

'The fact is, Margery, you can't sell illegal drugs to our members.'

'So you said last night,' replied Margery, not wanting to get into conversation again about this.

'Well it's true. I'm not going to prison for you.'

'No one is asking you to. It was just a few harmless plants. Chances are our members wouldn't have known what they were.'

'Did you sell any?'

'One or two.'

'Can you remember who you sold them to?'

Margery thought for a moment. There had been a lot of interest in her plants and it was difficult for her to recall who bought what.

'Well let's just hope they don't realise what they've bought. Do you grow many of them?' Edna was curious.

'A few. They seem to thrive in my conservatory as it is south-facing and they get plenty of light and at night I leave the light and a heater on.'

'What do you use them for?'

'Mostly pain relief, but some people just use them to feel good.'

'Well, just be careful. You're lucky it was me who discovered them and no one else, otherwise you could be in serious trouble.'

Margery ignored her as she had heard all she wanted to hear. She pulled out a cake tin and removed the lid. 'Fancy a piece of cake? This is my lemon and poppy seed cake.'

It did look delicious and breakfast had been a long time ago, but Edna didn't want to take any chances in case Margery had slipped any of her herbs in it.

'No thank you,' she declined.

'Are you sure? It does contain poppy seeds but not opium as such,' teased Margery knowing full well that Edna was not known to refuse a piece of cake.

'I'm absolutely certain,' replied Edna, realising that she had answered in haste and in effect had shot herself in the foot as she would have loved a slice, but she felt embarrassed to change her answer.

Edna looked around the kitchen at all the jars of dried herbs. She was amazed at the variety of jars that adorned the shelves. The door to the conservatory was open slightly and she could just about make out the sight of some of Margery's cannabis plants.

Margery noticed Edna looking. 'You're welcome to have a proper look.' Margery suspected that Edna was here to check her out rather than come to apologise.

'I was just curious.'

'Be my guest.'

The conservatory looked beautiful. More like a greenhouse than a conservatory with plants everywhere. There was little place to sit down, but there was something quite appealing about the room. There were about a dozen cannabis plants on the windowsills and in front of them on the floor were numerous other pots with a variety of herbs growing in them. Hanging down from the ceiling were bunches of herbs, drying.

Although Margery was definitely no drugs baron, Edna was impressed by the number of herbs she had.

'I heard that Gillian did a dem at flower club last month. Shame I couldn't get there,' Margery tried to divert Edna's attention.

Edna hesitated. 'Yes, she was good.'

'How's that fella of hers? Say anything about him?'

'What, her husband?' Edna was slightly confused.

'Well, if you can call him that. They're not actually married,' Margery let slip before she realised what she had said.

Edna had no idea and for a split second was quite shocked that Gillian and Charles were living together outside of Holy matrimony.

'It's a common-law arrangement. Gillian can't re-marry until they know for sure that Robert isn't coming back. Apparently you have to wait seven years before re-marrying,' clarified Margery.

'She said he was fine.'

'Huh. He's a right so-and-so. I keep telling her to get out of that relationship. After all, she just has to kick him out, but she won't.'

Edna was shocked by Margery's comment. 'Really?'

'Gillian's pretty unhappy but I don't think she wants to be alone.'

Gillian and Margery had known each other for years. They met through their husbands, or at least Margery's husband and Gillian's first husband.

Henry and Duncan had gone to school together and had kept in touch when they headed out to work. Before Duncan had met Margery he and Henry would often spend weekends together going walking. Henry, being the persuasive type, would occasionally drag Duncan to see a football match, although it wasn't really Duncan's style. He'd prefer to go walking in the countryside. Their lives changed to a certain extent when they both married, but they kept in touch and both couples would often go on holiday together. Gillian and Margery became close friends and discovered their mutual love for flowers. Not that Margery was particularly good at flower arranging but she was always happy to go and watch a demonstration or see a flower festival with Gillian.

Edna had no idea that Margery and Gillian were such good friends and was curious about Gillian's relationship with Charles, but she didn't like to ask Margery any more questions. She got the distinct impression that she had outstayed her welcome, and having been satisfied that Margery wasn't running a major drugs racket from her home, she made her excuses and left, still regretting that she hadn't tried Margery's lemon and poppy seed cake.

Polly awoke with a start and looked at the bedside clock. 'It's ten o'clock,' she shouted to Mark who was close to being unconscious beside her.

'What?' he grunted.

'It's ten o'clock,' she repeated.

He didn't know if it was the quantity of chocolate or the 'secret ingredient' but his head was banging.

'I knew we should have stopped at two slices. Trust us to be greedy.'

Mark turned over. 'Aren't you going to work? I thought you had some meetings today?' enquired Polly.

'I have, but there's no way I'm going in feeling like this. I'll phone in sick.'

'Well, that isn't a lie.'

'I haven't felt this rough since we went out for that dodgy Indian and downed a couple of cheap bottles of wine,' reminisced Mark.

'I know.'

Polly got up and headed downstairs to the living-room. What was left of the cake was on a plate on the coffee table. She looked at it and wished she hadn't eaten quite as much but there was no way she was going to throw out such an amazing cake. She knew she was being naughty by even considering eating the cake after knowing what was in it, but after a lot of discussion with Mark and trying to justify their actions they decided not to waste it. They certainly weren't disappointed but were paying the price today.

SEVEN

'Gillian, the police are here to see you.'

Gillian stopped what she was doing, having been surprised by what Charles had said.

She walked into the hallway to see two plain-clothed police officers standing there. 'Is there a problem?' she asked, curious as to why they were there.

'We'd like to talk to you about your husband, Robert Simmonds,' said the younger of the two officers. The very mention of his name caused Gillian's heart to beat faster.

Gillian showed them into the lounge and sat down. What with the subject of Robert being raised the other week when she did her flower demonstration, and now this, Gillian felt quite sick.

'Do you want me to leave?' asked Charles, although he was interested to know what the police had to say.

'No, stay please,' pleaded Gillian, pleased to have someone familiar with her even if it was Charles.

'We believe we might have found his body,' stated the older of the two police officers.

'Where?' Gillian was overcome with shock.

'A body has been found on the ship. We believe it could be your late husband.'

Gillian could feel herself trembling and she turned a pale shade of grey.

'What do you mean, you found him on the ship? How can that be? He disappeared nearly three years ago,' chipped in Charles, curious as to the circumstances of the discovery.

'I know it's incredible that he hasn't been discovered before now, but it would appear that he fell down a shaft and got wedged between the wall and some of the engineering equipment. There's no way anyone would have known he was there as this equipment only gets serviced every few years.'

Gillian was shocked. To think that Robert was on the ship all along.

'I hope he didn't suffer.'

'Initial post-mortem results would indicate a head injury of some sort, so chances are he would have died quickly,' surmised the police officer, aware that he wasn't fully in possession of all the facts but he had noticed Gillian was getting distressed.

'Do you want me to identify him?' she asked, innocently. Charles smirked at Gillian's naivety.

'That won't be possible, I'm afraid. Although he was protected, I'm afraid that his body has decomposed quite considerably, so it might be better if we identify him from a DNA test or dental records. However, we have also retrieved some jewellery that he was wearing. Can you identify this?'

The police officer showed Gillian a photo of the signet ring and prized cufflinks that Robert used to wear and had been wearing on that fateful evening.

'Yes, those belonged to him.' She trembled as she handed the photo back to the police officer.

'Do you still have anything of his that might have his DNA on that we can use to compare? If not, can you tell us who his dentist was and we'll get hold of his records.'

Gillian headed upstairs without saying a word. She opened the door to the spare bedroom and removed some of Robert's belongings that she hadn't the heart to throw out. She handed them to the police officer. Tears started to well up in Gillian's eyes. She had always assumed that he had fallen overboard as that was the only logical explanation, but the reality of the situation hit her hard.

Charles showed the police officers out and walked back into the lounge where he found Gillian slouched in the arm chair.

'Well, that's that then,' he said quite callously.

'What do you mean?'

'At least we now know that he's not coming back,' Charles replied, coldly.

Gillian thought back to that fateful cruise that she had looked forward to so much.

When Robert agreed to go on the cruise with her he was extremely concerned about it. Being on the ocean was not something that he relished but it was clear that Gillian had set her heart on going to the Bahamas as she loved going on cruises and this was somewhere she'd never been to before. Reluctantly, he agreed to go and went ahead and booked the trip.

'Aren't you excited about our holiday?' questioned Gillian, who couldn't understand why he was so negative about it.

'In a way I'm looking forward to seeing that part of the

world. But I don't travel well on the sea. I get incredibly seasick even going down a river on a boat,' he admitted, although he was known to be a bit of a hypochondriac.

Gillian suggested he went to see Margery to get some herbs to try and settle him down before the trip. Margery gave him one of her concoctions and told him to start taking it a few days before the journey. It made him feel a bit lightheaded and slightly tired but Gillian insisted that he would get used to it, so he persevered with it.

Whether it was physical or just psychological but Robert was feeling seasick almost before the ship had set sail. Initially Gillian was sympathetic, but this started to wear thin as Robert kept staying in his cabin, not wanting to venture out on to the deck as the cruise progressed.

There was some relief when they reached the Bahamas as Robert suddenly felt much better. Gillian finally started to enjoy the cruise with Robert by her side and it was everything she had hoped for. However, as they began the long cruise back home Robert started to feel ill again.

Gillian was sitting at the dining-table in the restaurant on her own. She looked around the room at all the couples laughing and enjoying themselves. Robert had taken to his bed once more, saying he didn't feel well. Despite taking the herbs Margery had prescribed for seasickness he still felt unwell most of the time. Gillian's dream of this being the perfect holiday was starting to turn quite sour for her as she had spent so much time alone.

'Mind if I join you?'

Gillian looked up. Standing beside her was a man around the same age as her. He had grey, thinning hair and a smile that seemed to illuminate the room. He was quite stocky, with a bit of a beer gut; quite the opposite of Robert who was tall and thin.

'Not at all,' she found herself saying.

'I'm Charles. Pleased to meet you.' He held out his hand.

'Gillian,' she replied as he took a seat next to her.

They chatted and laughed together and Gillian found Charles incredibly easy to get on with. The following day she bumped into him again, although she wondered if Charles had orchestrated the meeting as it was a bit too much of a coincidence.

The more Gillian saw of Charles the more she liked him. Robert was still spending more time in his cabin than outside and in many ways she wasn't looking forward to him being back to his old self. There was something very refreshing about Charles, who seemed so attentive and interested in anything and everything Gillian had to say. They had spent so much time together that some of the other people on the cruise were beginning to think they were a couple.

'Great news. I've got us a seat on the captain's table this evening at dinner,' announced Charles.

Gillian was so excited. This was something she could brag about when she returned home. The only fly in the ointment was Robert. He had been feeling slightly better that day with the help of some medication the ship's doctor had prescribed. However, Gillian didn't want anything to spoil her chance of sitting at the captain's table. She had to come up with a plan.

'I think I might be well enough to have dinner with you tonight,' Robert announced quite out of the blue. 'These new tablets are making me a little tired but I'm feeling much better.'

'That's good,' she lied. Gillian wasn't too sure how she was going to tell Robert that she didn't want to have dinner with him and that she had been spending time with Charles.

Robert slowly got dressed into his dinner jacket. He took out his favourite cufflinks from a box he kept in the cabin safe. They were bought for him by his first wife and he treasured them; something that Gillian felt extremely uncomfortable with.

She noticed his tablets sitting on the table. What if she gave him an extra tablet? she thought. She assumed that all that would happen was that it would make him more sleepy so that he didn't want to go out for dinner.

Part of her was against this, but her desire to have dinner with Charles was far stronger and without realising what she was doing, the next minute she was crushing one of the tablets and putting it into Robert's tea. He drank it without being aware of the fact that it had been drugged. Unbeknown to Gillian Robert had already taken a double dose of the prescribed tablets to guarantee not feeling seasick. Added to the combination of herbs that Margery had given him this had created a hallucinogenic cocktail that was ticking away inside him.

'I'm not feeling too well,' he said as he sat down on the bed, his teacup still in his hand.

'Why don't you have a rest for a while,' replied Gillian, trying to sound sympathetic.

Robert lay down on the bed. Everything was spinning and he closed his eyes. 'I'm not sure I'm going to be able to join you for dinner,' he muttered as he quickly drifted off to sleep.

Gillian had a slight pang of guilt, but nothing more. As far as she was concerned Robert would just sleep for the evening. She quickly got dressed into her favourite glitzy evening-dress, put on some make-up and headed off to the restaurant to meet Charles.

Charles looked quite dapper in his black tie and dinner jacket and he was impressed to see how amazing Gillian looked. They took their seats at the captain's table and spent the evening chatting and laughing with all the other guests.

The evening flew by and Gillian suddenly noticed the time. 'I think I'd better get back to see how Robert is,' she said to Charles.

'I'll walk you back to your cabin,' he said. Ever the perfect gentleman.

As they approached the cabin they noticed the door was open. Gillian walked inside but there was no sign of Robert. 'He's gone,' she called out to Charles.

'He can't have gone far,' he tried to reassure her. Charles had seen Robert on a few occasions so he had a vague memory of what he looked like. 'I'll go and check the restaurants and bars, why don't you go and have a look on deck,' he suggested to Gillian.

After an hour or so of searching there was still no sign of him.

'I'm sure he'll turn up,' said Charles. 'Leave it until morning and if he hasn't reappeared by then we'll alert the ship's crew.' He was mystified. He didn't think it would be possible for someone to just vanish from a cruise ship. Presumably Robert had got up and decided to go for a drink or something to eat. He left Gillian and headed back to his cabin.

A few hours later, when it was light, Gillian was banging on his cabin door.

'Who is it?' he called out.

'It's Gillian.' Charles got out of bed and opened the door.

'Has he turned up yet?' he asked, convinced that the answer would be yes.

'No he hasn't.' Gillian was clearly worried.

'Wait while I get dressed and we'll go and alert the crew.' He threw on an old pair of trousers and shirt and in a matter of minutes they were standing in the purser's office.

'When was the last time you saw him?' asked the purser who looked young enough to be Gillian's grandson.

'Last night just before seven. He wasn't feeling well. I left him asleep in our cabin.'

'When did you notice him missing?'

'Just after midnight. The cabin door was open but there was no sign of him.'

'We searched everywhere,' interrupted Charles.

'I'm sure he'll turn up. After all there's nowhere to go,' insisted the purser. 'I'll put an announcement out for him as soon as it's eight o'clock.'

'Why wait until then?' asked Gillian.

'It's a bit too early now. I'm sure there's a simple explanation but I don't want to wake up the whole ship at this time. Why don't you go and get some breakfast and I'll come and find you.'

'I don't want breakfast,' Gillian shouted. She was trembling. 'Where on earth can he be?'

'Come on, Gillian. Let's go and get a cup of coffee while we're waiting,' reasoned Charles as he led her out of the purser's office towards the restaurant.

'I'm sure he'll be fine,' he tried to reassure her while he got her a cup of coffee. While they were sitting there pondering where Robert could be the tannoy on the ship crackled into life as the purser made the announcement for Robert to go to his office.

Gillian and Charles got up and headed to his office in the hope of meeting Robert there. After half an hour still there was no sign of him.

'Can you make the announcement again?' asked Gillian. By now she was feeling extremely nervous and worried as to where on earth Robert could be.

The purser obliged. 'I'll also have a look at the CCTV to see if I can see him.'

He scanned through the various recordings on the ship and located Robert leaving the cabin around 11.30 p.m. He was clearly staggering as though he was drunk. The purser looked at the next recording taken from another corridor and was able to piece together the final moments of Robert's life. He finally found him standing on the deck around midnight. The image wasn't clear but he was convinced it was him. On one tape he was there, the next minute he had disappeared.

The purser looked concerned. 'What's the matter?' asked Gillian, clearly aware that something wasn't right.

'I'm not sure. I expect it's nothing. I'll be back in a minute,' mumbled the purser, who returned a short time later with the captain. He remembered Gillian and Charles from the dinner the previous evening and had assumed they were a couple.

'My husband's missing,' said Gillian as she saw him.

The captain looked confused. 'My husband, Robert,' clarified Gillian. 'Charles is just a friend of mine.'

He nodded. He wasn't too sure what the relationship was but he was more concerned that Robert had appeared on the deck one minute and was gone the next.

'We're going to conduct a full search of the ship for him. I want all crew to search this ship from top to bottom,' ordered the captain.

The search seemed to take an eternity but there was still no sign of Robert. It was then that the captain realised that something terrible had happened. The only logical explanation was that Robert had fallen overboard although in all his years at sea he had never known this to happen, and it certainly wasn't easy for someone to fall with all the safety precautions in place. But from the CCTV it did look as though Robert was disorientated.

All of this seemed such a long time ago but the visit from the police officers brought the memories flooding back to Gillian as though it was only yesterday.

While Gillian was sitting in her lounge pondering what had happened she looked at Charles. How smitten she had been with him and how selfish she had been to stop Robert from spoiling her evening. Guilt overwhelmed her and she burst out crying.

'It's all right, dear,' said Charles trying to comfort her, but his words came across as being insincere.

'No, it's not all right. While we were out enjoying ourselves he was dying.'

'We couldn't have known that.'

'I should've been with him. He wasn't well. I should've stayed with him and taken care of him. After all he was my husband.' She had never told Charles that she had drugged him.

'Well hindsight is a wonderful thing. At the time you wanted to sit at the captain's table. I didn't force you.' Charles spat the words out.

Gillian felt empty inside. She needed to get away from Charles so she could be with her grief, which in many ways had been put on hold since Robert's disappearance. She picked up her coat and headed outside to the car.

'You're in no fit state to drive,' Charles called after her, but his words were unheard.

Margery was busy tending to her plants when Gillian arrived. 'Is everything all right?' she asked when she saw Gillian pulling up on to the drive and getting out of the car. She looked flustered and had been crying, judging by the redness around her eyes. Gillian didn't answer her but burst into tears as she reached the doorway.

'What on earth's the matter?' asked Margery, somewhat taken aback by Gillian's behaviour. She had rarely seen Gillian cry over anything.

'They think they've found Robert,' she spluttered.

Margery looked at her. 'What, is he alive?'

'Of course not.'

'Well, I only wondered.'

'They've found a body. They assume it is Robert. They're going to try and do a DNA check on him, but they found his ring and cufflinks with the body.'

'Where did they find him?'

'Can you believe it? He was on the ship!'

'What do you mean, on the ship?'

'Just what I said. He died on the ship. Fell down a lift shaft or something like that.'

'And they've only just found him? How can that be? Surely someone could smell him.'

Gillian was slightly taken aback by Margery's question. The

thought of smell hadn't even entered her mind. 'I suppose so,' she replied. 'They said he was wedged somehow between a wall and an engine or something like that. No one noticed him.'

For a split second Margery could see the funny side on this. 'What, no one noticed a dead body?'

Gillian wasn't in the right frame of mind to be remotely amused. All she could think about was her guilt for what she had done.

'That's incredible. Surely it must be Robert. After all, how many dead bodies are there on the ship.' Margery was still pondering the situation. 'Does Charles know about this?' she continued.

'Yes, he was there when the police arrived.'

'And?'

'He was his usual uncaring self. He almost seemed relieved that Robert was definitely not coming back.'

'Surely you've realised this for some time?'

'Not really. I suppose that as there wasn't a body I always wondered if there was a chance that he might still be alive. That somehow he fell overboard and was rescued. I really miss him.' By now Gillian was rambling.

'Come and sit down and let me make you a cup of tea, or would you like something stronger?'

'Tea is fine.'

Margery handed Gillian a cup. She took a sip of it and proceeded to spit it out. 'What on earth is that?'

'I put some sugar in it. After all, you've had a terrible shock,' explained Margery. Clearly Gillian didn't appreciate having three spoonfuls of sugar put in her tea.

'What if I had something to do with his death?' asked Gillian, almost too afraid to get the words out.

'Why do you say that?'

'I secretly gave him a dose of his medicine. I drugged my own husband. What if this drug plus your herbs made a lethal combination?' Margery didn't respond.

Margery thought for a moment. It was true that she had given him one of her herbal concoctions and although on its own she didn't think it would do much harm, combined with some 'proper' drugs there might well have been a reaction.

'He was staggering on the CCTV, like he was drunk or something.'

Margery knew that Robert never touched a drop of alcohol so his behaviour could well have been caused by the drugs.

'I'm sure you had nothing to do with it,' said Margery although she wasn't totally convinced. 'Why on earth did you sneak him a dose of his medicine?'

'I wanted to be with Charles,' confessed Gillian. 'I didn't want Robert to go to dinner with me that night as I so wanted to sit on the captain's table with Charles.'

'Oh,' replied Margery. She might have guessed that Charles had something to do with this, albeit indirectly. She had no time for him and had strongly advised Gillian not to let him move in with her, but as she was so enamoured by him her words fell on deaf ears.

'You're not going to marry Charles now are you?' Margery suddenly felt worried for Gillian.

Gillian glared at her. 'That's the least of my worries right now.' She started shaking and tears welled up in her eyes again. 'What have I done?' Gillian was inconsolable.

'Try not to worry about it. It's not as though anyone will ever find out that you gave him the extra dose of medicine.

After all this time I doubt the police will be able to test for anything much.' Margery tried to reassure Gillian, although deep down she was concerned about her own prescribing of herbs and whether they could be implicated in his death.

'I'll try not to.'

'When will you know for sure if it is Robert?'

'They didn't say. They took some of Robert's belongings with them to get a DNA match and said they'd be in touch as soon as they'd had a chance to test the body. I don't know why they're wasting their time on this. It's obvious that it's going to be him. If they found his cufflinks and signet ring it can't be anyone else.'

Gillian sat quietly for a while, deep in her thoughts. Margery allowed her to ponder. After a while Gillian appeared slightly more relaxed. 'How's Charles?' Margery dared to ask.

'Same as ever.'

'Just be careful. I don't trust him. I get the feeling he's just after your money. Don't be talked into anything right now.' Margery felt herself lecturing Gillian.

'Don't worry, I won't. Things aren't great between us at the moment. I found him going down my purse the other day, and when I checked our joint account I noticed he'd spent a large sum of money.'

'See, I knew he was up to something.'

'What on earth would he need so much money for?'

'Did you ask him?'

'He said it was a surprise, but nothing has been forthcoming. I've got a feeling he might be gambling again.'

'If I were you I'd change the bank account so he can't get his hands on your money. You shouldn't have set up a joint account.'

'Yeah, well that's easy to say. Hindsight is a wonderful thing, but at the time it seemed the most logical thing to do.' Gillian sighed. 'Right now I wish so much that Robert was still here.'

'He had his moments though, didn't he? And those dreadful children of his.'

'Yes, you're right. I suppose I should tell them that they might have found Robert's body.'

'Wait until you know for sure. You never know how they'll react.'

Margery was probably right. After all, they had tried to get her evicted on more than one occasion since Robert's disappearance, so once they knew for sure that their father was dead it would be hard to predict how they would respond.

EIGHT

Cynthia had been flower arranging for years. Her mother was a flower arranger, as was her grandmother, so she grew up with flowers in the house and had a natural flair for it.

Despite her family's background in flower arranging it was only after Cynthia's marriage failed that she took it up as a hobby at her mother's insistence. It wasn't long before she realised that this was a lifeline for her. Whilst she hated the idea of joining clubs, she soon realised that unless she took up floristry professionally, something she had no desire to do, she needed to join a club to further her skills. She discovered a flower club not far from her house and became a member.

For years she would turn up at the meetings each month and participate in the various shows. However, she was aware that they were always looking for people to go on the committee. For some reason committee members at her club seemed to come and go with great regularity.

After a lot of persuasion she agreed to join the committee in the role of press officer. She knew there were very different personalities on the committee and some of the longer serving members seemed to run things, but at the time it didn't bother her. It was only when several members resigned as they felt they were being stifled by some of the other people on the committee that she agreed to take on the role of chairman in the hope that she might be able to turn things around.

Things didn't go according to plan and, despite having a lot of new ideas to move the club forward, there were constant objections from the old-timers on the committee who didn't want to move into the present age. Everything became a battle and when challenged the committee members soon showed their true colours and turned on Cynthia. They didn't want someone who was going to question the way things were done or try to change anything.

Cynthia thought of herself as an extremely assertive and resilient person; someone who was not a push-over, but the constant challenge of her decisions and back biting and bitchiness took their toll. As a result Cynthia felt she had no option other than to resign and later decided to leave the club for good and start all over again. After all, flowers played such an important part in her life, it was just some of the people she couldn't cope with.

After that she kept a low profile and perhaps this was why she was never asked to do anything. So the call from the area chairman to invite her to be on the show committee for the upcoming flower show was fantastic for her. This was her chance to shine and she was determined to make it a success.

The meeting was held in Diane's house. Even though Cynthia lived in a reasonably large house, Diane's seemed to eclipse hers. The lane to her house was somewhat dark and, despite the spectacular views, Cynthia was pleased she didn't live there. She had never been one to cope with darkness and isolation. She very definitely liked to have a streetlight outside her front door.

She pulled onto the drive behind a couple of other cars that were parked there and rang the doorbell. The door was opened by someone who she didn't recognise.

'Hello, I'm Cynthia. I've come for the meeting with Diane,' she said, slightly nervously in case she had the wrong house.

'Come in. I'm Vivienne,' came the reply. She was shown into the conservatory where several ladies were sitting, all with a cup of coffee and helping themselves to biscuits. Cynthia introduced herself to everyone before Diane appeared at the doorway.

'Thank you for coming,' Diane opened the meeting. 'I'm pleased to be able to tell you that the venue has been confirmed and I've put together an information pack for you all.'

Diane handed out some official-looking packs that outlined the show and what was expected of each of the people on the show committee. Cynthia quickly glanced at the pages and noticed her name was on several of them.

'I suggest everyone has a read of these,' instructed Diane. 'I've put together various job functions, and what our objectives are for the show.'

Diane had worked most of her life as a secretary and was used to organising people and events. In many ways she was a natural choice for staging an event on this scale. She noticed a look of surprise on Cynthia's face. 'Cynthia. I'd like you to manage the competition in the main marquee.'

'Really? That would be great,' replied Cynthia, somewhat taken aback by the level of responsibility she was being given.

'Any problems, please let me know,' insisted Diane, who was determined that this would be the best show ever, especially as it was the last show she would be organising whilst in her role as chairman.

'Vivienne, you are arranging the tombola and raffle.'

'You do know I'm competing in the show too?'

'Yes, of course. That's not a problem. I suggest you find a few helpers to get the tombola set up while you're doing your exhibit,' she suggested.

There were general sounds of agreement as the other ladies read what their responsibilities would be, and Diane outlined them in more detail.

'Let's hope we don't have any cheating this year.' Diane was hopeful there wouldn't be a repeat of the last show.

Cynthia's ears pricked up. 'Cheating?'

'Last time we had a show one exhibitor entered four classes and won all four,' filled in Vivienne.

'What's the problem with that? They must be really good to get four first places.' Cynthia was puzzled.

'Not really. Every design was copied from a book or magazine. In fact one of the designs was mine. I had it photographed and published in a magazine,' said Vivienne, stating the facts.

'You're joking. That must have shocked you when you saw it?' Whilst there is no truly original design as everything has been done before, Cynthia was shocked by what she heard.

'Nope. I'm not joking. When I saw it I couldn't believe my eyes. It looked exactly how I did it originally.'

'Didn't you tell the judge so that she was disqualified?'

'Couldn't. None of them recognised the design so she got away with it. Mind you, afterwards I did tell her what I thought. I'm not aware she has competed in any shows since then, thank goodness.'

'Well, let's make this the best show ever,' said Diane. 'One other thing,' she remembered a point she needed to raise with the committee. 'If you're watering anyone's exhibit, please make sure the spray bottle you use is clean.'

Cynthia raised her eyebrows.

Vivienne started laughing. 'I'd forgotten that. One of the committee sprayed a number of exhibits as it was very hot that year. The problem was that her husband had previously filled the spray bottle with weedkiller and hadn't washed it out. Needless to say, the following morning half of the flower arrangements in that class were dead.' She explained to Cynthia.

The committee burst out laughing.

'Exactly. We don't want anything like this happening again, and certainly not on my watch,' reiterated Diane. 'Any problems, let me know, otherwise I'll see you at the showground on set up day.' Diane concluded the meeting.

Cynthia left the meeting feeling extremely pleased with herself and excited about the forthcoming show. Who would have thought that she would be given a task like this after everything she had been through?

NINE

After Polly had got so excited about the possibility that Gillian might have murdered her husband she still hadn't had time to research the strange disappearance of Robert. She had been so caught up with sorting out her design that this ended up firmly on the back burner for a while.

Having mocked up her design and had a few sleepless nights worrying about it she decided she needed to make a few changes. The stand was fine. It was her choice of flowers and colours that she started to question. Having so many gerbera and chrysanthemum in it made the design look somewhat unbalanced and flat, so she set about trying to find an alternative flower that would make her design flow more readily and bring it to life.

The day was fast approaching for the show and she was getting nervous about everything. She even started to question her design. In the quiet hours of the night her mind would be flitting from one thing to another, usually ending up with wondering what Amy was doing. How had Amy interpreted the brief? Would Polly's design be good enough or was she going to make a fool of herself as this was well out of her comfort zone? Would her flowers survive for a few days with limited water supply? Would the judges think that she had a good enough variety of textures or should she introduce another plant material? Had she interpreted the design correctly or should she have stuck with her first idea? She wished her brain would switch off but the self-doubt was relentless.

Polly always went through this before a show, and this show in particular as it was so prestigious. Every time she told Mark that she would never put herself through all the stress again. 'This is the last time I'm competing in this show,' she would say to him. 'Next year remind me about how ill I'll feel and that I shouldn't do this to myself.' Mark would just nod and agree with her. He had heard it many times before and always knew that the minute the competition schedule for the show was out Polly would be excited about entering. Negotiating with her not to compete was not an option for him as he knew he would get nowhere. 'I don't know if my stress levels will cope with doing this again, but I must. It's like a drug,' she would say to him, trying to find an excuse for going back on her word.

'Never mind your stress levels. What about mine? I'm not sure I'm up to going through it all again,' he would reply, half joking and half serious. He hated seeing her get so stressed about anything, although he knew that she seemed to thrive on it.

'Just popping out.'

Mark looked curiously at Polly. 'Where are you off to? I thought you were in tonight?'

'I just need to get some foliage for my design.'

'What, in the dark?'

'Yes. I thought I'd wait until there's no one around.'

'So you're nicking stuff?'

'Not exactly. I'm doing some community pruning.'

Mark smiled. 'Same thing.'

'No it's not. I'm doing the community a favour by trimming back overgrown foliage.'

Mark tutted. 'Just don't get yourself arrested.'

Polly was a bit nervous about going along the path in the dark but she didn't want anyone seeing her cutting the foliage so she didn't have much choice. Even though in her eyes she was doing nothing wrong a part of her felt slightly guilty.

She had noticed the ivy when she had cut through the housing estate to the shops the other week and it was exactly what she needed for her design. She always made a mental note of where she had seen different plant material, just in case she needed any. It wasn't unknown for her to knock on someone's door and ask if she could cut some foliage from their garden. Most times they agreed to let her do this, although some looked at her as though she was mad. She had only had a problem on one occasion when the resident gave her a long-winded lecture about her garden and then shut the front door in her face.

Polly approached the overgrown ivy and began cutting a few branches from it. She wasn't too fussy with what she cut, partly because she couldn't see too well in the dark. She put the branches into the black sack she had with her. When she felt she had cut enough she turned round to head for home.

Standing in front of her was a police officer. 'Can I ask what you're doing?' he said.

Polly suddenly felt extremely nervous and guilty. 'Just trimming some of the ivy,' she stuttered.

'Have you sought authority to do this?'

Polly hesitated for a second. 'Not exactly.'

'You are aware that this is council property.'

'Yes.'

The police officer looked at her.

'Yes, I do understand whose property it is but I don't think that I'm stealing as such. I'm doing the council a favour.'

He wasn't totally convinced. 'What do you intend to do with it?'

'I need it for my flower arrangement.'

'Is this for your own use?'

'I'm entering a flower competition.'

'My wife does flower arranging.'

'Oh really? Well, I'm sure she would understand.'

'I'm sure she would.'

'So are you going to arrest me or what?'

'No, but be careful. You were reported by a concerned resident who saw you.'

'What, they thought I was a burglar?'

The officer ignored her question. 'There have been a few break-ins recently so everyone is keeping their eyes open for suspicious behaviour.'

Polly hadn't realised that cutting a few pieces of ivy would cause a problem, but with hindsight she understood exactly where the residents were coming from. Seeing someone sneaking around in the dark with a bin liner was bound to arouse suspicions.

She walked back to her house as quickly as possible, clutching her bag of ivy.

'You've been ages. I thought you were just walking to the

alley at the end of the road,' Mark said as soon as she opened the front door.

'I did go there, but I nearly got arrested.'

'You what?'

'A policeman arrived. Someone reported me. They thought I was a burglar.'

Mark laughed. 'So instead of doing community pruning, you're now doing community service?'

'No. I told him I was helping the council by trimming back the ivy.'

'Bet he was impressed with that explanation. What did he say?'

'His wife is a flower arranger.'

'I might have guessed.'

'I bet she does community pruning too.'

'Probably. I see he let you return with your contraband.'

'Yes. He just told me to be a bit more careful in future.'

Polly took the ivy out and put it in a bucket that she placed on her back doorstep. She'd inspect the ivy in the morning for any wildlife that she had inadvertently picked up. Then all she had to do was sort out the flowers she had collected from the wholesaler and pack her sundry items, and she was ready for the show.

'You'll never get all that stuff in the car,' noted Mark.

Polly glanced at all the boxes strewn across her living-room floor. She did have a lot of 'stuff' but competing at a show at this level meant she had to take additional flowers and lots of sundry items, just in case.

Mark looked in one of the boxes. He laughed. 'Why on earth are you taking this?' He pulled out a child's dustpan and brush; the head of the latest cartoon character was on the top of the brush handle.

Polly looked up. 'I need that to sweep round my design.'

'Yeah, but how embarrassing to be seen with something like this.'

'I know,' Polly smiled, 'but at least no one's likely to pinch it, or if they do I'd be able to track it down.'

Mark pulled another item from the box and shook his head. 'I'll never be able to understand this flower arranging lark. Seems like old junk to me.'

'That's because you don't understand art,' Polly said with a laugh.

'While we're on the subject, I see you've taken over the cupboard in the spare room with your "art".'

Since Polly took up flower arranging she had pretty much taken over the whole house. Her collection of 'art' filled the loft and any spare cupboards. It was even a struggle manoeuvring the car into the garage in between pedestals, vases and odd branches of wood.

'Can't we get rid of some of this junk? It's getting ridiculous,' Mark had asked when he looked in the garage one day.

'You never know when I might need it,' was Polly's reply.

'What, even this old stick?' Mark had said, laughing as he held up a broken piece of wood in his hand.

'I bet if we get rid of it, I'll regret it.' Polly knew her collection of bits and pieces was getting slightly out of control to the point of her becoming a hoarder but she had no intention of downsizing.

Polly was still rummaging through boxes, trying to memorise what was in each box to make life easier for her when she got to the show, and the nervous energy kicked in.

'Can you help me load up the car?' she asked Mark, who had by then settled down to watch rugby on the television.

'OK.' He reluctantly dragged himself off the sofa. Anything for a quiet life.

They made their way the car and started loading it, carefully packing each box and bucket of flowers into the space like a complicated mosaic.

'See, it did fit,' remarked Polly, feeling quite smug with herself. There was just about enough room for her in the car. She started up the engine and wound the window down. 'Wish me luck.'

'Good luck.' Mark waved as he headed back in the house for a quiet afternoon while Polly went to set up her design.

Polly moved the car a few yards down the road before noticing something wasn't quite right. The car felt different from usual. She pulled into the kerb a short distance from her house. She got out and walked around the car, inspecting it.

She stood still, looking at one of the tyres in disbelief. It was as flat as a pancake.

She ran back to the house. 'Mark, Mark,' she called out. 'It's a disaster. The tyre's flat.'

Mark rushed to his feet and followed her to the car. 'Yep, you're right, the tyre is flat.' He stated the obvious.

'Can you change it for me? I've got to get to the show now otherwise I won't have time to set up my design.' Polly was starting to panic. She was nervous enough about competing in this show and now her whole world was threatening to come crashing down around her. Tears started to fill her eyes.

Mark looked at her and placed a hand on her shoulder. 'It's OK, it's only a puncture.'

'You don't get it do you? I've got to get there, all the work and stress I've had over this design,' she rambled.

'Well, I'm afraid we've got to unload the car so that I can get to the spare tyre.'

They painstakingly began removing all the items from the boot. It took considerably less time to unload the car than it had to load it and it wasn't long before the entire contents were standing on the pavement beside it.

As expected Amy had everything packed up and ready to go long before she needed to even though set up time didn't start until two o'clock. All her materials were in specially purchased boxes and all neatly marked. Her toolbox was filled to capacity with every tool she would ever be likely to need. Even the buckets for her flowers all matched perfectly.

She lived by her philosophy of if it is worth doing it is worth doing well. There were no short cuts as far as Amy was concerned, even if it would save Malcolm's bank balance from taking a battering on a regular basis.

Malcolm was outside preparing his car for the journey. He put the seats down in the back and covered them with a protective plastic so that they didn't get damaged in any way with Amy's buckets and boxes.

Amy took all her boxes out to him and he painstakingly started loading them one at a time, being extremely careful. Amy always found this quite difficult to watch; if it was down to her she would have them loaded in a matter of minutes, but Malcolm never liked to rush such a complicated process as this. To him it was an art form. He wedged one or two of the boxes with old towels so that they didn't fall over on the drive to the showground.

Not wanting to get in the way, Amy headed back into the house to do one last circuit to check that she had taken everything she needed with her. She had turned up for a show once and realised that she had left her toolbox behind on the kitchen table. Malcolm had to drive home at a rate of knots in order to pick it up and get it to her so that she could do her exhibit. He hadn't been particularly pleased about this and Amy didn't want to go through this experience again.

Once convinced that she had all the essential items in the car she locked up the house and sat in the passenger seat while Malcolm did one last check of the stability of the boxes before closing the boot and setting off.

By the time Mark had put the spare tyre on and they had repacked the car, Polly was in a real state. She felt consumed by panic.

'I can't believe this is happening to me,' she said, feeling incredibly stressed by the whole affair.

'It'll be fine. Just be careful driving there. You've still got plenty of time to get there.'

Polly wasn't really listening to him. 'What?'

'I said, be careful driving there. You're clearly on another planet right now. I'll sort the tyre out tomorrow. Just drive carefully and try not to worry.'

Mark gave her a quick peck on the cheek as she got into the car. He stood and watched while she drove off down the road before heading back in doors to watch the rugby, hopeful that there wouldn't be any more disasters that afternoon.

TEN

After what had started as an eventful journey, the rest of the drive to where the flower show was being held was fairly straightforward with little traffic. Polly managed to make up lost time and as soon as she arrived at the showground she headed to the area of the marquee where she would be setting up her exhibit. Having located her name on the floor she was dismayed to see that Amy was not only competing in the same class as her but was situated next to her. Her heart sank.

Her thoughts were interrupted by her phone ringing.

'Get there OK?' enquired Mark, having felt slightly nervous for the past hour wondering if Polly was all right.

'Yes, thank God. No more problems, though you'll never guess what.'

'What?'

'Amy is competing next to me,' she said in a hushed voice.

'Don't let her intimidate you. You're just as good as her if not better. Just do your best and I'm sure everything will be OK,' Mark tried to reassure her.

He was probably right. After all when it came to flower arranging you never knew how things were going to turn out. Flowers are a medium that you can never rely on no matter how many times the design has been mocked up before a show.

Polly had to make several trips back and forth to her car to unload all her 'stuff' and it wasn't long before it was crammed in round her in the tiny space she had been allocated.

Amy arrived. As usual she was giving out her orders to Malcolm. He unloaded all her flowers while Amy stood around looking to see who else was competing in the show. She spotted Polly and just about managed to squeeze out a 'hello' after looking her up and down, clearly unimpressed at being positioned next to her.

It was a huge marquee featuring a number of different flower arranging classes. Several smaller marquees in the grounds had other competition classes and retail stalls selling a variety of items, some of which, no doubt, would end up in Polly's garage.

Polly set about putting her vision into reality. It took a considerable amount of time doing all the preparation work and assembling the spheres. She was a little concerned that they took far more flowers to cover than she had expected. Having painstakingly assembled these giant spheres with chrysanthemums, Polly tied strong fishing line on to a wire that she had placed through the centre of each one. She had tested these when she mocked up the design and was happy that the fishing line could take the weight of the spheres so she felt confident this wouldn't cause a problem.

Before attaching the spheres to the stand she decided to go for a wander round the marquee. Partly because she was nosey and wanted to see what other exhibitors were doing but it had been a long time since she'd had a cup of tea and she was desperate for a drink.

She headed to the tea urn that was placed on a table at the side of the room. There were teabags in an old plastic box and the table was covered in spilt tea, sugar and dirty teaspoons. It was hardly appealing but Polly was gasping and having located a new polystyrene cup she dunked a teabag into a cup of hot water. There were a few broken biscuits left on a plate for exhibitors to take. Polly picked up a couple of pieces and decided to go in search of Sarah who was also competing in the show.

Sarah didn't relish doing the huge designs that Polly loved to do, so she was competing with a much smaller flower arrangement in one of the other marquees that was nearby. It wasn't long before Polly had located her.

Sarah's design was coming along nicely. 'What d'you think?' she asked.

'Looks lovely,' Polly replied, genuinely impressed by Sarah's work. Sarah had a really unique way of interpreting the class titles.

'Does it depict the Silk Road?'

'Yes it does. I love the colour you've used,' observed Polly, looking at all the reds and oranges.

'The poppy heads represent the fact that opium travelled along this route. The fresh and dried millet symbolises the fact that the road starts in lush areas, but ends up in the desert. Then of course there's some silk which is self-explanatory,' Sarah explained.

'I'm not sure the judges will look that deeply into the interpretation. But I think it deserves a first prize.' Polly gave her opinion knowing full well that Sarah would have given the design a lot of thought in the planning stage, although sometimes she felt she did over-think her designs.

Polly looked around the marquee to see if there was anyone she knew and noticed Jennifer setting up a few tables away. Jennifer was a member of the same flower club as Polly and although they weren't particularly friends, they knew each other. Jennifer was exhibiting in the same class as Sarah. Polly went to investigate and say hello to her.

It was a strange design. Jennifer had a heart of gold and was so enthusiastic but in reality she didn't have a creative bone in her body. From Polly's point of view the design was unbalanced and some of the flowers had clearly seen better days, but at least she was having a go.

'How's it going?' asked Polly, not too sure what else to say about the design.

'It's fine. I'm really pleased with it,' enthused Jennifer.

'You've used some interesting plant material,' Polly said, not wanting to burst her bubble. She recognised some familiar leaves. A voice in Polly's head screamed to her, 'OMG!'

'Yes, aren't these leaves lovely? I bought this plant from Margery's plant stall at club the other week.'

'Lovely. Well, good luck with it.' Polly made her excuses and made a hasty retreat back to Sarah, not wanting to get into too much of a conversation over the plant material.

'You'll never guess what,' she whispered in Sarah's ear. Sarah looked at her enquiringly.

'She's only got some of Margery's cannabis in her design,' said Polly, with a laugh.

'You're joking. Well you could say it's authentic. After all a lot of drugs were transported along the Silk Road.' Sarah paused, her conscience starting to kick in. 'Should we tell her?'

'No, she's well chuffed with it. She'd be mortified if she has to dismantle it.'

'But if she gets disqualified I'll feel dreadful.'

'Maybe the judges won't even notice,' insisted Polly, fully aware that they probably would and that Jennifer might find herself in trouble. 'What's happened to the woman next to Jennifer? The one with wet hair and a wet shirt?' she asked Sarah.

Sarah burst out laughing. 'You know the giant trough they fill up with water for us to soak our floral foam in?'

'Yes.'

'Well, she fell in.'

'No.'

'Yep. She went to soak her floral foam and dropped it in the trough, and while she was trying to retrieve it somehow she slipped and went head first into the trough.'

Polly couldn't believe her ears. She had almost done this herself when she managed to drop a block of floral foam and saw it sink to the bottom.

'I went out there about ten minutes after her and all I could pretty much see were her feet sticking out. She was hanging over the edge trying to retrieve a giant block of foam and next minute there was a splash. I had to help fish her out!'

Polly was crying with laughter. 'How funny.'

'It was. I really had to try hard not to laugh. A few of us managed to get her block of foam from the bottom of the trough while she went and got dried off. I can't believe how heavy floral foam is when it's wet.'

'I can't believe she tried to soak such a huge piece of foam in a trough that's three foot deep.'

'I don't think she'll be doing that again. Don't you need to get back to your design? Not wanting to hurry you or anything.'

'Yeah, best get back and start assembling mine now that all the hard stuff has been done. See you later.' Polly made a quick exit from the marquee.

There were a large number of competitors in Sarah's class as it was obviously a popular title for a flower arrangement. Sarah was setting up next to Hilda, an elderly lady she did not know but had seen her exhibit at other shows.

Hilda was busy putting the finer details to her design. Whilst her arrangement was somewhat old fashioned it had a certain quality about it that Sarah liked.

'Are you married dear?' Hilda asked Sarah, totally out of the blue.

'No. Never found the right person.'

'I know a lovely man who is looking for a girlfriend.'

'Really?' Sarah wasn't too sure whether or not to take her seriously.

'He's good-looking. Has his own house. Quite a catch I think.'

It wasn't clear to Sarah if Hilda was after him or if she was doing a bit of matchmaking. By Sarah's standards and experience with men, he sounded quite appealing.

'And he's financially secure,' continued Hilda, trying to sell the idea to Sarah.

'Out of curiosity, how old is he?' Sarah enquired, half serious.

'I believe he was eighty on his last birthday,' Hilda replied in a very matter-of-fact way. It was only when the words came out that she realised what she had said.

Sarah roared with laughter. 'Well, if he can cut the grass and put the bin-bags out I'd still be interested.'

Hilda laughed. 'I suppose he is a bit too old for you.'

'More than a bit, I'm afraid,' insisted Sarah. 'I'm looking for someone about half that age.'

'Sorry, dear, I didn't think about that. I just want him to be happy and you seem such a lovely girl.'

Sarah was flattered that Hilda referred to her as a girl. 'Well, I'm sure if he's that nice he'll find someone.'

Sarah took another look at her design. Whilst some of the flowers hadn't behaved themselves the way she wanted them to she was fairly happy with it and set about putting the finishing touches to it. Draping the silk fabric along her design was proving more of a problem and she kept putting it on and taking it off.

'Better with or without?' she asked Hilda.

'Definitely better with,' Hilda confirmed, so Sarah had another attempt at placing the fabric without ruining her design.

Polly was still sniggering about Jennifer's design and the woman who had fallen in the trough as she arrived back in the main marquee. She walked past Maggie, who was setting up her exhibit further down the line. Her design was looking fabulous.

'Looking good,' Polly commented as she passed her, although not wanting to get into a discussion as she was keen to get her own exhibit finished. It was surprising how quickly time seemed to fly by when setting up a design.

Polly decided to start assembling her exhibit from the

bottom upwards so that it didn't become top-heavy and unstable. It took slightly longer to complete than she had planned but she wanted to make sure it was perfect. After she had tied the final sphere to the top of the design Polly took a few steps backwards to inspect her handiwork. It definitely had the 'wow' factor. Its vibrant colours and interesting textures would surely secure her a top prize, or so she thought.

Amy watched as Polly put the finishing touches to her design. Whilst she was loath to admit it, she thought that perhaps this time Polly would beat her.

The design was huge and with no upper height limit the exhibit seemed to tower over Polly. She noticed an area in the top arrangement that needed a slight adjustment so she took out a small folding footstool to stand on so that she could reach it.

Suddenly there was a strange sound above her and she noticed the top sphere starting to move towards her as the strain on the fishing line became too much for it. In a split second the sphere fell on to Polly. It took Polly by surprise and knocked her off balance. Polly grabbed at her exhibit, trying to regain her balance, but all that did was make her even more unstable and she fell off the footstool, taking her design with her. One sphere flew off the top of the design and headed straight for the exhibit that was being set up next to her. This exhibit was unstable in its own right and the impact of the sphere catching the over-height branch in the design caused that to topple and create a domino effect, taking down the next design too.

Maggie saw what was happening and quickly positioned herself to the side of her exhibit. She managed to catch the pedestal from her neighbour that was heading towards her and saved her own design from becoming yet another victim.

There was a gasp in the room as everyone stopped what they were doing and looked over.

'Polly, are you OK?' Maggie called out. There was no reply. Maggie didn't dare move while she was supporting her neighbour's pedestal.

Polly lay still, winded, covered in wet floral foam and flowers. Every bone in her body seemed to ache and she didn't want to move.

Sarah had decided to pay Polly a visit. From across the room she saw her design, which looked amazing, but in that split second it was in a heap on the floor. She rushed over to her.

'You OK?' Sarah asked, genuinely concerned.

'I think so,' replied Polly, who was on the brink of tears.

'Take your time before you try to move,' advised Sarah.

Amy looked at her pristine design, untouched by the carnage. A wry smile appeared on her face. She was pleased that Polly had fallen in the opposite direction and avoided knocking her design over.

With only an hour to go before the official setting-up time ended and judging commenced, Cynthia decided to do another circuit of the show area to check progress. Everything was coming along nicely with some fabulous designs, or so she thought until she entered the main marquee.

She could see a group of people congregating along one side of the marquee. She pushed her way through to see what all the fuss was about and was greeted with the sight of three exhibits lying in tatters on the floor. One of the exhibitors was in tears and another was stomping around in fury.

Cynthia noticed a body sprawled on the ground under one of the exhibits. Flowers and floral foam covered them and she deduced that this was where the problem began.

Polly didn't want to get up. She felt mortified by what had happened and was aware of the fact that she had an audience. Amy, not wanting to get involved and believing that she now stood the best chance of winning, continued assembling her design.

Sarah glared at her. 'The least you could do is help.' Amy ignored her.

'I know my design was stable,' insisted Polly. 'I bet she sabotaged it.' She looked in Amy's direction.

'Don't think about it right now. Do you think you've broken anything?'

'What, apart from my stand?'

'Yes. Any broken bones?'

'I don't think so.'

Sarah took one of Polly's arms, and Cynthia the other. Between them they helped to raise Polly to her feet. Sarah picked off some of the plant material that had lodged itself firmly in Polly's hair.

'I don't believe it,' cried Polly when she saw her wonderful design trashed. She noticed the damage she had done to the other exhibits and felt extremely guilty. 'I'm so sorry,' she said to the two competitors who were by now picking over their designs in the hope of salvaging something to present to the judges.

Cynthia surveyed the area. 'I'm sure we can sort this out,' she said, trying to restore calm. 'Let's clear away anything that is unusable and see what is left.'

Sarah retrieved the guilty sphere that had travelled such a distance, causing so much destruction in its path.

Surprisingly, it wasn't too damaged. Just a few missing flowers; definitely something that could be repaired.

Polly looked dismayed. Tears started to well up in her eyes.

'Come on, Polly. You can do it,' encouraged Sarah.

'I haven't got time to re-assemble everything.' Polly felt helpless.

'I don't think you have to. Look.' Sarah showed her the sphere. 'Just a few modifications and you'll be fine.'

'But it's all ruined,' insisted Polly.

'No it isn't. I'm sure it is salvageable. You just may not be able to do exactly what you had planned. I've got some flowers left over that you can use and I'm sure other competitors can let you have any spares they have.'

Sarah stepped over to where Cynthia was standing. 'Is there any way these ladies can have a bit more time?' she pleaded.

'Rules are rules, I'm afraid,' stated Cynthia.

'I know they've still got an hour left but surely it's better to give them a bit more time to repair their exhibits rather than having this huge gap. We want to put on a great show for the public,' Sarah said, reasonably. She had a point. After all these were extraordinary circumstances.

'Leave it with me. I'll see what I can do although I'm not promising anything.' In a split second Cynthia was hotfooting it to the judges' office.

Polly gathered up her stand and examined it. There was no way she could recreate her original idea but Sarah was right, with a bit of thinking outside the box she should be able to display something. Whether or not she would want to admit that it was her work was yet to be seen.

'Stephen will be mortified,' said Maggie as she was inspecting the damage. 'The last thing he wants is for one of his stands to fail.'

'I don't think it did. Something broke or came detached. The only reason it fell was because I knocked it,' insisted Polly.

She looked at the wire that had attached the top part of her design to her metal stand.

Interesting, she thought. 'Look at this.' She showed Maggie the wire, which seemed to be neatly cut through. She glanced in the direction of Amy, sensing that Amy was watching her. Amy started fumbling in her toolbox.

Polly noticed a pair of wire cutters under her hand. She seemed to be trying to hide these.

'That's convenient,' Polly implied.

'What do you mean?'

'Well, someone has cut through my design and you've got a pair of wire cutters.'

'That doesn't mean anything. I bet a lot of people have got wire cutters in their toolboxes.' Amy had a point, after all Polly had some too.

'Whatever,' snapped Polly.

'If you're accusing me of sabotaging your design, prove it.'

'I will, don't you worry.' Polly was feeling herself getting angry but knew she had to try and calm down if she wanted to create something for the judges.

'You're mad. Why on earth would I do that? You're no competition to me, I always beat you fair and square.' Amy spat out the words just as Cynthia returned.

'When you've quite finished, ladies,' Cynthia intervened, 'I've got good news. The judges can let you have an additional half-hour.'

'That's not a lot of time,' observed Polly.

'I'm afraid that's the best I can do.'

'I'm assuming I get the extra half-hour too?' enquired Amy although her design was already more or less complete.

'No, only the three ladies who've had their exhibits damaged.'

'That's not fair,' protested Amy.

'These are rare circumstances and an extra thirty minutes might mean the difference to being able to have three more designs rather than a huge gap,' she said, reiterating what Sarah had said.

'I'm going to make a formal complaint about this.'

'You do that,' retorted Cynthia. She had met Amy's kind before and she was determined to stand her ground with her. Polly smiled inwardly. Judging from the way Amy was stomping around, she had definitely met her match with Cynthia.

Amy was furious. She bundled up all the remaining flowers into buckets and threw her boxes in the back of Malcolm's car.

'Everything all right, dear?' he reluctantly asked, fully aware that everything was not all right. Usually Amy left a flower show with an air of confidence. Her behaviour on this occasion was a first for Malcolm.

'No it isn't,' she snapped while she forced the boxes into the car.

'Careful with that.' Malcolm pointed to where the paintwork of his car had been scuffed by the box.

'Stuff your bloody car,' Amy erupted as she got into the passenger seat, leaving Malcolm speechless. He'd never seen her like this before and didn't dare ask her what had happened until she had calmed down a bit.

Polly and the other two ladies who were having to rebuild their designs worked at breakneck speed, and it wasn't long before they were putting the finishing touches to their designs thanks to the generosity of other exhibitors who all readily gave them unwanted flowers and plant material to use.

Sarah waited to check that Polly was OK before she left. She could see that Polly had once again been able to come up with a top notch design and was amazed to see that it was more or less finished.

'I don't know how to tell you this, Polly,' she said.

'What?'

'I think it looks better than the original.'

Polly took a few steps backwards so that she could get a better view of it. She wasn't totally convinced. Her eyes immediately went to all the faults. She had spent so many months planning this design but to see that it didn't look like the image she had in her mind was frustrating for her.

'Are you all done?' enquired Cynthia, keen to clear the area so that the judging could begin.

'Thank you for your help and understanding,' Polly replied.

'Not at all, Polly. Good luck.'

Sarah helped Polly load up her car with all her boxes and Polly headed for home for a well-deserved rest.

Mark was still up when Polly arrived. He could tell immediately that things hadn't gone according to plan. She looked tired and distraught as she opened the door.

'Well?' enquired Mark.

Before Polly could get a word out she burst into tears and nuzzled her face into Mark's neck. He let her cry for a while before prising her off him and looking her in the eye.

'Oh, Polly, what's happened?'

'It was dreadful. The whole day has been a disaster.'

'I'm sure it's not that bad.'

'Amy sabotaged my design.'

Mark looked shocked. 'What do you mean?'

'My whole design collapsed. I bet Amy had something to do with it.'

'Are you sure?'

'Well, one minute everything was fine, the next minute I was hit on the head by a sphere of chrysanthemums, knocked off my footstool and my whole exhibit came crashing down on top of me.'

'No!'

'That's not the worst of it.'

Mark was beginning to see the funny side of the story but tried not to show it. As Polly recounted the story she too started to laugh as it seemed such an outrageous situation.

'The sphere somehow bounced off my head then crashed into the exhibit next to mine. That fell over taking the next exhibit down with it too.'

Mark was laughing in disbelief. 'I wish I'd been there. This sounds hysterical.'

'Well, it wasn't.' Polly tried to stop laughing but her tears of anger and frustration had turned into tears of laughter as the stress from the day was released.

'What was the class called?' asked Mark, fully aware of the title.

Polly could barely get the words out. 'Balancing Act.'

Mark pulled a face at her. Polly tried to ignore him but couldn't and the two of them were crying with laughter.

'And I wore my lucky socks. Fat lot of good they did

me.' She pulled off the pair of bright orange and lime green spotted socks and tossed them in the rubbish bin. 'Sarah said that she thought my revised design looked better than the original,' she continued.

'Is that a compliment?'

'Not sure how to take it. That my work looks better once it's been trashed and reassembled.'

'Did Amy's exhibit get smashed up?'

'No. Sod's Law that the flying sphere went in the opposite direction. Her exhibit escaped the carnage. She was really miffed when I was told I could have a bit longer to assemble my design. She said she's going to complain. Silly cow.'

'I don't know why you get so stressed with all this. After all it is just a bunch of flowers. It's meant to be fun.'

'Not when the likes of Amy are involved. As far as I'm concerned, this is total war now. I'm sure she cut the wire holding my design together.'

'Yeah, but you haven't got any proof, though, have you?'

'Not exactly.' Polly didn't actually have any real proof but she didn't want to admit that she might have done something wrong. It was much easier to blame Amy.

'Then I think you've got to let it go – put it down to experience,' reasoned Mark.

'I suppose so. I'm going to bed. I've had just about enough of today.'

Mark suspected that she would not let it go and that this saga was likely to continue for weeks if not forever.

After a long period of silence Amy started ranting about the afternoon, blinking back the tears of anger. She was furious. Malcolm tried his best to calm her but it was no good.

'How dare she accuse me of sabotaging her design,' she spat out. 'The fact is that she designed it badly so that it toppled.'

'I expect she was upset about it collapsing and lashed out at anyone, rather than accept it was an accident,' Malcolm suggested.

'Don't take her side.'

'I'm not. I'm just saying.'

'You just don't understand,' interrupted Amy, not wanting to hear what Malcolm had to say on the subject.

'I think you just need to forget it. There's no point in making yourself ill over this. It is what it is.'

But Amy was in no mood to think things through logically. She could already feel a migraine coming on and all she wanted to do was get indoors and go to bed.

ELEVEN

Polly had a restless night as her dreams kept taking her back to the afternoon's proceedings. The only difference was that in her dream she had completely trashed Amy's design.

She lay awake, a wry smile on her face as she remembered her dream. It was funny how the subconscious plays out how we really feel, she thought. Her stomach churned. She always felt nervous after a competition, wondering if her exhibit was still standing; if the flowers were still alive; if the judges liked it or not. But on this occasion she was worried about the design she put forward. She was convinced she wouldn't win anything or that some other catastrophe had occurred.

Mark was up early. He popped out first thing and sorted out a new tyre for the car, then came back and started to get breakfast. He'd already got the kettle on and bread in the toaster as Polly made her way downstairs to the kitchen.

'Cuppa?'

'Please.' Polly stood in the doorway. 'I'm dreading going

back to the show. I don't suppose you'll go on ahead and tell me if it's OK for me to go in?'

'Don't be silly. We'll go together and have a look. If you don't go you'll get even more stressed. I'll be there with you and we can face the result together,' he said, reassuringly.

Mark was right. The worst thing was not knowing how she had got on but she hated going into any show until she knew if she had won anything. She needed to prepare herself for a bad result so that she didn't get too upset or make a fool of herself if she was disappointed.

As soon as they had finished breakfast they headed off for a fairly uneventful drive to the show.

When they arrived at the showground they were directed along a narrow lane to the carpark which was in fact one of the surrounding fields. The ground was very wet underfoot, having had so much rain overnight.

'I hope we don't get stuck in the mud,' commented Mark as he noticed areas that were completely waterlogged.

Polly didn't respond. She was too tense to hold any normal conversation. Her mouth had completely dried up with nerves. Mark held out his hand to her, which she took without hesitation and they walked slowly towards the marquee.

'Just remember, it's meant to be fun, all this flower stuff,' insisted Mark, well aware that Polly was likely to be very upset if she came away from the competition with no prize.

'I'll be happy with anything right now. Just as long as I've won something,' she said, although deep down she was still hoping for a good result despite everything.

They walked into the marquee. Polly showed her exhibitor's badge and was let through immediately but Mark had to pay his entry fee. Polly walked on ahead of him, unaware that he wasn't right behind her. She glanced into the area where her design was. She could feel her heartbeat getting faster and stronger. She took a deep breath.

'It's still standing at least,' she said over her shoulder to Mark, who was by now just a few paces behind her. She was suddenly excited as she could see a card of some sort on the floor in front of her exhibit.

'There's something there. I might have won a prize,' she said excitedly, realising that this show might not be the disappointment she had been expecting.

Polly was so focussed on the card in front of her exhibit she didn't notice Sarah standing there. Sarah had a big smile on her face. 'Come and have a look.'

'I can't. What does it say?' asked Polly, a short distance away.

'You've come first,' Sarah announced to her.

Polly couldn't take it in. 'No way, what does it really say?'

'You've got the first prize. I wouldn't be so cruel to tease you about this.'

Tears welled up in Polly's eyes. She started shaking. 'I don't believe it' she kept saying. 'I thought it was crap.'

'I told you it looked great.'

'Well done, Polly, it looks beautiful,' said Cynthia as she walked past.

'I just don't believe it,' repeated Polly as Mark caught up with her. 'I've won first prize.' Tears streamed down her cheeks with relief and excitement.

'That's fantastic news. I told you not to worry, didn't I? Just goes to show that your lucky socks were lucky after all.'

'I'll have to fish them out of the bin. Remind me the minute we get home. I'd hate for them to be thrown away.'

Mark nodded. 'How did your "best friend" get on?'

Polly glanced over at Amy's design and started laughing. 'She got nothing. I've beaten her in style this time.'

Amy arrived at the marquee. Dressed in her newest designer outfit, with matching handbag and shoes, she made her way across the room. She had calmed down from yesterday afternoon. An air of arrogance convinced her that she had probably won the competition. From the sound of hearing her name being mentioned and the reaction of people as she walked past she assumed this to be true. It even crossed her mind that she might have won the 'best in show.'

As she got close to her design she looked around the floor to see if there was an award card. There was nothing. She assumed it must be tucked over the other side of her exhibit. She checked all around her design for a second time but there was definitely no award card, just an envelope. She opened the envelope to read a standard printed letter that stated that her work had not been deemed good enough to win an award. Included in the envelope was also a comment card from the judges: 'Lovely flowers but the design is unbalanced and overfull. Fewer flowers would have given the design more shape.' She was shocked and humiliated. 'How dare they say this?' she asked herself. She could feel anger rising in her. She glanced over at Polly's exhibit next to hers and saw the group of people photographing it. It was then that she noticed that Polly had come first.

'This is an outrage,' she shouted. 'That woman cheated.'

By then she had an audience. 'She was given extra time to complete her design. That is totally unfair and unacceptable.' But no one seemed particularly interested and assumed it was just sour grapes. She could see Polly was surrounded by people congratulating her. Polly, surprisingly, refrained from commenting although she really felt like saying something, but her shock of coming first stopped her from doing this. No one was going to spoil this special moment for Polly.

Amy continued to direct her barrage of abuse at Polly, but all it did was make her look stupid.

Malcolm had finally managed to park the car in an area that wasn't too muddy and was not far behind Amy. There he found her shouting at everyone and looking bright red. She was furious. He correctly guessed that things hadn't gone to plan.

'Stop making a scene.' Malcolm tried to calm her down but this made things worse. 'You're making a fool of yourself. Just accept it gracefully. Let's get a cup of tea,' he suggested. He always hated being the centre of attention and Amy's behaviour was almost too much for him to bear, with everyone looking at her and talking about her.

Amy stood looking at her design. She could not believe that she hadn't won anything. To make matters worse, she noticed that the two other ladies who had been given extra time had also won prizes, in fact hers was the only exhibit in that class that hadn't won anything. She swung round with such force that her handbag flew off her shoulder, catching one of the arrangements on her stand and sending it flying. Malcolm picked up her handbag from amongst the flowers and led her out of the marquee to the tea room without examining the damage she had done. The last thing he wanted was for Amy to be scrabbling around on the floor picking up the flowers that had fallen out of the arrangement.

'Congratulations,' shouted Lizzy as she saw Polly across the marquee.

Polly was still beaming.

'Well done, Polly, you've done us proud,' said Edna.

'It's not how it should be. Everything went wrong.'

'That doesn't matter. The fact is that it looks stunning and it's wonderful that someone's given Amy a run for her money.'

'I guessed something had happened when I saw Amy shovelling a large slice of cake and then a cream scone in her mouth in the tea room. Malcolm looked shocked and embarrassed. Not sure if it was because this was the most food he's ever seen her eat, or what,' said Lizzy laughing.

'You shouldn't be that cruel, Lizzy,' commented Edna, although she secretly agreed with her. She glanced at the design next to Polly's. 'That one's dreadful. Whose is it?'

Polly laughed. 'That's Amy's.'

'No. Is it supposed to look like that?' asked Lizzy looking at the broken flowers on the ground.

'Put it this way, Amy and her design had an argument,' Polly explained.

'That must have been one heck of an argument.'

'Well, it was quite funny. She was so angry when she saw I had beaten her and that she hadn't won anything that she flew into a rage and her design got damaged. One of her placements got hit by a flying handbag. That's what all those flowers are.' Polly pointed to the scattering of flowers on the ground and the bald piece of floral foam on one of the stands.

Edna started to laugh. 'You've really had an interesting time of it, haven't you?'

'It started badly with the puncture. Then there was the

collapse of my design with the flying sphere. In the end everything worked out perfectly for me despite the flying handbag. I'm so chuffed. Still can't believe it.'

Sarah was beaming. 'You deserve it, Polly, especially after what happened yesterday. I think your design is amazing.'

'Me too,' agreed Edna. 'How did you get on, Sarah?'

'Great, thanks. I came second in my class which I'm happy with. The one that came first was stunning.'

'I'm assuming it wasn't Jennifer's?' asked Polly.

'No, the judges commented that they weren't happy with some of her plant material.'

'I wonder what on earth they could mean by that,' queried Edna.

Polly laughed. 'It might have had something to do with the fact that she put some cannabis leaves in her arrangement.'

Edna looked shocked. She knew that a couple of members had purchased the plants from Margery's plant sale, but didn't know who exactly. She wondered if the cannabis saga would ever be over.

'Plus someone tried to set me up on a blind date,' commented Sarah.

'So a good result all round then?' questioned Mark.

'Sadly I turned the date down. I know I'm desperate but not that desperate to go out with someone twice my age!'

'Well at least neither of us fell in the water trough,' added Polly.

'You what?' asked Mark.

'That's another story completely,' said Sarah, with a laugh.

TWELVE

After the euphoria of coming first in the flower show, Polly was starting to come down to earth and refocus on other things, until her next big flower competition which was a few months away, then the whole process would start again. She had been so caught up with her design for the competition that for a while she had completely forgotten about Gillian. Now that she had a quiet moment she settled down in front of her computer in order to try and get to the bottom of her suspicions about Robert's disappearance. Not too sure where to begin, she tried searching on the Internet for Robert. It wasn't long before she came across an article about the strange happenings on the cruise.

According to the article Robert had consulted the doctor whilst on the cruise as he wasn't feeling too well. The doctor diagnosed nothing more than seasickness and prescribed some medication that was known to cause drowsiness and confusion. Some of the passengers noticed him one evening on deck. It looked as though he was drunk as he was unable to walk in a straight line. No one saw him after that. It was only when Gillian raised the alarm after she found that he was not in their cabin when she returned from having dinner one evening that panic started to kick in. A thorough search had been made of the entire ship, but there was no sign of him. CCTV was on the deck area, but with the darkness starting to creep in it was difficult to make out much detail from this, other than a black figure on the deck one moment and not there the next.

The ship was sailing near the coast of Spain on its way back from the Bahamas. The local coastguard sent out boats to search for Robert as soon as it was light enough, but there was no sign of him, or any remains for that matter. The article continued that Robert left a wife and two children from a previous marriage.

There was nothing particularly suspicious by the sounds of it. Polly felt somewhat disappointed by the article as she was desperate to find some juicy gossip.

'I had a go at researching the death of that chap on the cruise,' announced Polly when Mark returned from visiting the local shops.

'What, the husband of your flower lady?' enquired Mark.

'Yes.'

'And?'

'Well, nothing really. Sounds like he wasn't well and the doctor gave him some medication that might have affected his balance. No one knows what happened to him but logic would say he'd fallen overboard.'

'So it was just an accident then?'

'Suppose so. What a disappointment.'

Mark smiled. 'Trust you to be disappointed at that.'

'I was just hoping to uncover something interesting.'

'Poor guy. What a way to go.'

'Yes, that is pretty gruesome, isn't it? To be drowned and eaten by fishes,' Polly surmised.

'Not nice. Hope I don't end up that way,' replied Mark, feeling quite concerned.

'Well, at least he was on his way back from his holiday so he'd had a nice time and good memories.'

Mark laughed. 'You have a funny way of looking at things, Polly. Would it have made it any better if he wasn't on his way home from his holiday?'

'I'm just saying, at least he had …' Polly paused. She knew what she wanted to say but she seemed to be digging a deeper hole for herself, judging by the expression on Mark's face.

He laughed. 'I know what you mean, Polly. I'm just messing about. Trust you to try and find a positive out of such a terrible situation.'

Polly wasn't expecting to see Sarah today, but as she looked out of her kitchen window she noticed her pulling up in front of the house. She opened the front door and called out to Sarah as she got out of the car.

'Hello. This is a surprise.'

'What are you doing? Fancy going out?'

'OK.' Polly didn't have much planned for the day now that she had finished her research into Robert's disappearance.

'I've found a lovely new tea room.'

'Really, where's that?' Polly was starting to get interested.

'Just down the road from you. It's called the Carlton Tea Room.'

'Oh, that one. I've driven past it loads of times but never been in. What's the cake like?'

'Lovely. And they have lots of talks and demonstrations there.'

'Anything particular?'

'There was someone in there the other day doing a talk about the local history. Quite fascinating.'

'Were there many people there?'

'About thirty. It was really packed.'

'It must've been.' Polly knew how tiny the tea room was.

'It was really funny. I wasn't sure if I'd get a seat. It was full of really old dears and I was too afraid to take any of them on. They were all pushing past me to grab a seat.'

Polly laughed. 'Only a brave person would take them on. These old folk, they're pretty scary at times. Did you get a seat or did you end up having to stand?'

'Amazingly, I got a seat. I spotted a spare seat on one of the benches in the room, so I threw my jacket over the heads of people in the queue in order to grab it. It landed spot-on. I think some of them were a bit surprised when they saw my coat appear from nowhere but at least I had somewhere to sit.' Sarah smiled, recollecting the event and the reaction of some of the people when her coat flew through the air on to the bench.

'What was the talk like?' asked Polly.

'Part of it was really interesting. I had no idea about the history of this area, even though I've lived here for the last twenty or so years. Some of it got a bit boring, though.'

'Anyone nod off?'

'Most seemed to be quite caught up in it. I think I was the only one beginning to nod off! Anyway, they're having a talk about plants this afternoon that sounds just up your street.'

Polly wasn't sure.

'It's about poisonous plants. I think the talk is called "Who Dunnit?"'

'Now that does sound interesting.' Polly's mind raced back to Gillian and her husbands. Even though she had not found out anything unusual about Robert's death she was still convinced that something untoward had happened to him.

'Not that you need any more convincing but the entrance fee offers you a free cup of tea and a piece of cake.'

'Decision made, then.'

'Are you OK to go now? Parking's a bit of a pain round there.'

'Just popping out with Sarah.' Polly shouted out to Mark. He wasn't particularly bothered as he was used to Polly disappearing at short notice.

'OK, see you later,' he replied, quite half-heartedly.

Polly grabbed her handbag, and her coat which was hanging in the hallway. 'Just a second,' she said. She returned with a notebook and pen.

Sarah gave her an inquisitive look.

'Well, you never know. I might need to make some notes.'

'OK, Miss Marple.'

'Didn't find out anything exciting about Gillian,' Polly said as she got into the car.

Sarah smiled. 'I wondered if you'd be investigating her.'

'Well I had to. After all, I hate not knowing what happened.'

'So, is that the end of this now?'

'Definitely not. I'm sure she had something to do with his disappearance. I only need to figure out what exactly.'

Sarah glanced over at Polly. She looked miles away in her own little world of conspiracy theories.

Sarah pulled up in front of the tea room. As predicted it was difficult finding a parking space. 'I'll drop you off here and you go and grab some seats while I park the car. I'll have a cup of tea and a slice of their chocolate fudge cake, please.'

Polly did as instructed and entered the tea room. There were already quite a few people in there and she was glad that Sarah had dropped her off. A few more minutes and they would have ended up having to sit right at the back of the room. A couple of seats were still vacant in the front row so Polly pushed her way down the extremely narrow gangway that had been left in between tables and chairs and put her coat on them. She then went back to join the queue for the tea and cakes.

Polly's mouth watered as she saw the selection of cakes on offer. Decisions, decisions, she thought. This was an unexpected treat for her. She had planned on starting her diet again today, something that she tried to do most days, and once again, she was thwarted. Willpower was something she didn't possess much of and it didn't take much for her to stray off the path. She looked in the glass cabinet at the selection of cakes. Should she try the chocolate fudge cake, or the cherry and coconut, or the coffee walnut? For a split second she felt slightly panicked at being put on the spot.

'One ordinary tea with milk, and one weak black tea, please,' she ordered from the young girl who was working extremely hard behind the counter, trying to keep up with demand.

'What cake would you like to eat?'

'A piece of chocolate fudge cake and I'll try your cherry and coconut, thanks.'

Pleased that she had managed to make the decision

without getting too flustered after all, and relieved to see Sarah entering the tea room and joining her, they carefully carried their treats back to their seats.

Sarah glanced behind her. The room was packed once again with local people all eager to support the tea room and hear the talk, although some she suspected were just there for the tea and cake.

A man stood in front of them. He was in his sixties, had thinning grey hair, and the most impressive moustache which seemed to curl round at the ends. He gathered up various notes and picked up the microphone. He tested it and after almost deafening everyone with various screeches and buzzing sounds he was able to get the volume right, providing he didn't move round too much.

'It's nice to see so many people here,' he started. A loud screech filled the air. 'Sorry about that.'

'It's your tiepin. The metal is affecting the microphone,' pointed out Polly. She was used to trying to sort out the sound system at flower club meetings as the demonstrators often had problems with their metal stands and containers setting it off, and she had become quite knowledgeable over the years.

'Thank you. My name is Frank Smith and today I'm going to tell you things that will shock you!' he continued, having removed the tiepin.

Polly raised her eyebrows.

He began his talk. 'Did you know that your gardens are potential crime scenes? Whilst flowers are lovely to grow and have in the house many plants are poisonous to humans, and some are so deadly that they can kill.'

This was exactly the sort of information Polly was after.

Frank fired up the old projector. It was the same one that they had used at the other talk that Sarah had attended. As there were no curtains in the tea room the image on the screen wasn't very clear but they could just about make out various plants.

Polly was aware that a lot of plants caused problems, usually skin irritation, one such being euphorbia, which was the main culprit. But she was hoping to hear something a bit more shocking than this. She wasn't disappointed as the next plant appeared on the screen.

'Aconite is very poisonous to humans. If someone is poisoned by aconite it is difficult for a coroner to detect it as it clears the system after just a few hours. The poison is contained in the roots and, going back in history, it was used on the end of spears and arrows to kill prey. One of the names it has is wolfbane and it is reported to have been used to kill wolves. You can also be poisoned by picking the leaves. The poison acts extremely quickly, so if you think you've come into contact with it and start to experience feelings of numbness or nausea, etcetera, consult a doctor immediately.'

Polly was shocked. 'I use this in my flower arranging,' she called out.

'A lot of people do. It has beautiful purple flowers, but just be careful when you're handling it,' Frank reiterated.

'So can a human die from it?'

'Oh yes,' he replied with a somewhat worryingly smug look on his face, as though he relished the possibility.

'Have there been any reports of people being poisoned?' enquired Polly.

'There have been accidental poisonings with people handling it and not realising the dangers. As far as murdering someone with a plant, there were reports of someone being killed by it. Apparently their partner put it in their dinner.'

Polly couldn't believe her ears. Gillian must have done something like this, she thought.

'And here is the deadliest of plants, the castor oil plant.' Frank interrupted her thoughts.

'I've got one of those growing in my garden,' contributed one of the attendees.

'Me too. Why is it so deadly?' an elderly woman sitting at the back of the room asked, clearly concerned that she might be harbouring a murderer.

'The seeds are highly poisonous. It only takes one or two seeds to kill a human.'

There was a gasp.

'It's true. The funny thing is that it would take ten or eleven seeds to kill a dog and around eighty seeds to kill a duck!'

'I'm going to dig mine up. I don't want anyone dying,' said the woman, clearly concerned about having it growing in her garden.

'As long as you are aware of the dangers, it's fine. They're beautiful plants and extremely architectural in the garden,' Frank said with his horticulturist hat on.

'I do hope I haven't shocked you too much. Gardening is a wonderful thing and I would hate to put anyone off enjoying their garden. Just be careful out there,' Frank concluded his talk. He was given a round of applause and people started to head out of the tea room.

Sarah knew that Polly was well and truly fascinated by Frank's talk. She hadn't even finished eating the last mouthful of her cherry and coconut cake which was still sitting on the plate in her lap.

'That was amazing,' she said, beaming at Sarah. 'Thanks for inviting me.'

'You're welcome. Are you going to finish your cake, or what?' Sarah asked, wanting to clear her plate away.

Polly hadn't realised there was still a mouthful of cake left. 'This cake was delicious,' she said as she put it in her mouth and handed Sarah her plate and empty mug to put on the counter.

'Thanks for such an interesting talk,' she said to Frank, who was busy gathering up his belongings.

'I'm glad you enjoyed it.'

'It's such a fascinating subject.'

'Do you do much gardening?'

'Not a lot as my garden is small and very full, but I am a flower arranger so I'm used to handling lots of plant material.'

'Well, it's worth knowing what is and what isn't safe to handle. You don't want to make yourself ill with it.'

'Definitely not.'

Sarah looked at Polly. 'Ready to go?'

Polly nodded. She would have liked to have spoken more to Frank but didn't particularly want to divulge to him her reasons for her questions. After all, these were only her suspicions at this stage.

THIRTEEN

'Leave those hamsters alone.'

'I can't help it. They're so adorable.'

Polly had offered to look after her neighbour's hamster while they were on holiday. The slight complication was that the hamster had produced a litter of twelve a couple of weeks earlier. Polly was obsessed with them.

Mark sighed. He didn't want Polly getting too attached to them as the last thing he wanted was a cage of hamsters in the house.

'Look. I can hold all the babies in one go,' she said as she picked up a dozen sleeping hamsters. 'A bundle of hamsters. Aren't they the most beautiful things you've seen?'

Mark wasn't totally convinced about this. He accepted that they were cute. All had fur and their eyes were just starting to open. They felt nice and warm where they had all been sleeping together with their mum. In a day or two they would all be leaving the nest.

'Put them away or you'll be late for your committee meeting.'

Mark was right. Polly was due to pick Sarah up this evening and she didn't want to keep her waiting. She put the handful of babies back in the nest so that their mum could take care of them. After a quick inspection in the mirror to check her make-up and put on a bit of lipstick she was ready to go.

'See you later,' she called out to Mark.

'Don't come back stoned,' he replied. Polly smiled. The last meeting had been rather outrageous.

She picked up Sarah who was waiting for her. Sarah looked excited about something.

'Everything OK?'

'Yes.' Sarah smiled. 'Got myself a date!' she continued.

'Who with?'

'You remember that website I registered with?' Polly nodded. 'Well, someone called Colin contacted me. He sounds really nice.'

'And?'

'He works as a gardener and is a fellow vegetarian. I thought this sounded promising.'

'Do you know anything else about him?'

'Not really. He likes walking, plants and alternative medicine.'

'Well, at least he's not eighty, like the fella Hilda tried to set you up with.'

'Let's hope not. Just my luck I'll turn up and find that he's lied about his age.' Sarah hadn't had much luck with blind dates in the past.

'When are you meeting him?'

'Not for a couple of weeks as he's away now and then we're off to Winchester for the flower festival. Going to meet him at the garden centre. Was a bit nervous about going out in the evening with him in case I don't like him and need to make a quick exit.'

'Very wise. At least it'll be daytime and a public place so that if it all goes pear-shaped you can escape.'

Sarah was incredibly pretty, had a slim build and a lovely personality. Polly couldn't understand why she couldn't find that special person. Any relationship she had always ended in disaster. Perhaps it was because of Sarah's kind personality but men seemed to take advantage of her.

Sarah was already nervous about the meeting but Polly's comment made her feel even more worried. She tried not to dwell on it. 'Wonder if there'll be any excitement at the meeting tonight.'

Polly smiled. 'Who knows what will happen.'

They soon arrived at Edna's house and followed the usual procedure of leaving their shoes in the porch. Polly had remembered to check her socks before heading out this evening and although her socks were quite outrageous in their design, green and cerise stripes, at least none of her toes stuck out.

The other committee members were already sitting at the table ready to begin the meeting as Sarah and Polly were slightly late due to Polly not wanting to put the hamsters back in their cage.

'Right, ladies. Nice to see you all here tonight,' Edna opened the meeting. For once all committee members were present and the room was slightly crowded with additional chairs being brought in from other rooms to accommodate everyone. They raced through the first few points on the agenda.

'Who's our demonstrator this month?'

'Vanda Monroe,' replied Julia.

'Has anyone seen her before?'

'No, but I've heard she does some amazing work.'

'Any special requirements?'

'She says she wants to get into the hall at 6 p.m., but I've told her she can't get in until 7 p.m. She wants a ham salad sandwich on brown bread, no butter, with a little mayonnaise.'

'Oh, does she?' Edna was taken aback by the request. This was the first time a demonstrator had been so self-important and demanding.

'Who does she think she is? This isn't a restaurant,' commented Polly.

'I'll go and pick up something from the supermarket, though I doubt it'll fit her specific criteria.' Edna decided to deal with the situation herself as she could see her committee were unimpressed.

'She'll just have to lump it.'

'Thank you, Lizzy, for that comment.'

'Do all flower clubs provide the amount of catering we do for their demonstrators?' asked Sarah.

'It is fairly standard for flower clubs to do this or at the very least offer a cup of tea and a biscuit, but she really does appear to have taken our hospitality to the extreme,' admitted Edna, who didn't have time for prima donnas at the best of times. 'On to Lorna's garden party.'

Edna had put a vase of flowers on the sideboard next to where Polly was sitting. The scent from them made Polly sneeze. She felt in her sleeve for a tissue. She was sure she had put one there earlier but it seemed to have fallen out of the sleeve and further into the loose blouse she was wearing, which was tied at the waist by a belt. She gently tried to ease it upwards and out of her sleeve. As she started to do this something felt strange. This didn't feel like a tissue, it felt quite squidgy by comparison. Suddenly panic filled her. What had she got in her blouse? She was unaware that by then the talking in the room had stopped and everyone was looking at her, curiously wondering what was wrong.

Gently and cautiously she eased the object up inside her blouse so that she could pick it up. Then the realisation set in as she heard a faint squeak. She'd managed to take one of the baby hamsters with her to the meeting. She looked up and saw that she was the centre of attention.

'I'm afraid I'm going to have to leave the meeting,' she stuttered. 'I've managed to bring a baby hamster with me.'

The committee members looked at her in disbelief. 'A hamster?' asked Edna in a somewhat high-pitched voice.

Polly put her hands on the table, still cupped and enveloping the baby hamster.

'Let's see.' Barbara was curious. Polly opened her hands to reveal the adventurous creature.

'Ah, isn't he gorgeous,' came the response. 'He's so tiny.'

'Well, we've never had a hamster attend our committee meeting before. This is definitely a first,' observed Barbara.

Everyone burst out laughing. 'Are you sure there aren't any more hamsters hiding?'

Polly had a quick look but was satisfied that she had only walked out with one of the babies. 'It must've fallen down the top of my blouse when I was handling them earlier. Thank goodness I decided to wear a belt with this blouse. It must've got trapped by it otherwise it could have dropped all the way through. I feel quite ill thinking about what might've happened. I could have dropped him anywhere.'

'How are you going to get it home? Do you need a box or tissue to put it in?' asked Edna quite concerned about the welfare of the little hamster.

Polly thought for a second. She was afraid that the baby's body temperature might drop so she opted for the best solution. 'Don't worry about that. I'm going to put him in my bra and drive home with him there.' The committee weren't too sure what to make of this. First of all Polly arrives with a hamster down her top, then she drives off with him in her bra.

'Whatever next?' said Edna, somewhat amused by the whole situation.

Everyone was still laughing at the turn of events. 'Never a dull moment at our meetings,' observed Sarah, still unable to believe that Polly could have possibly driven there with a hamster secreted in her blouse.

'I think I should minute this,' said Barbara, with a grin.

'What are you going to put?' asked Lizzy, through tears of laughter.

'The meeting was interrupted by the sudden discovery of a hamster.'

'How about we had a gatecrasher,' suggested Julia.

'I think we should have a look around just to make sure Polly didn't bring in any more of her friends.' Edna was concerned that her cat might discover a tasty treat.

Everyone had a look around the floor and under the chair that Polly had been sitting on.

'Are we satisfied we are vermin free?' asked Julia.

'It could only happen to Polly,' Sarah laughed, knowing that the funniest things always seemed to happen to her.

'I think I might take this opportunity to get the kettle on. We don't want Polly to miss anything important.'

'Are we going to have some more of your delicious chocolate cake?' asked Julia, totally oblivious of the saga that had accompanied the happy cake last month.

Edna hesitated. 'Not tonight, I've made us a good old fashioned Victoria sandwich.' She didn't want to take any chances with any new recipes and had opted for something she knew well. There was no way she was going to get her committee stoned again.

By the time Edna had made the tea and returned to the meeting with it Polly was back.

'That was quick.'

'I literally just dropped him off and came straight back. Don't think the mum had noticed anything.' She laughed. 'Although Mark thought I was completely mad. Left him laughing.'

'Whose hamsters are they?'

'My neighbour's little girl. Can you imagine what would've happened if they'd come back and I was one baby short?'

'Doesn't bear thinking about. Still at least you have averted a complete tragedy. Have a piece of cake to calm yourself down.' Edna offered the plate.

Polly looked at Edna, a question in her eyes.

'Victoria sandwich this evening, my usual recipe,' Edna said, second-guessing what Polly wanted to know and relieved that Polly didn't make any comments about the cannabis out loud.

'Did I miss anything?' asked Polly, hopeful that the conversation about Lorna's garden party might have been completed by the time she had returned.

'No, Polly, we waited for you to get back,' Edna said,

unaware that this was the complete opposite of what Polly had hoped for.

'Now where were we before we were interrupted by the appearance of our unusual guest? Oh yes, Lorna's garden party.'

'Lorna has asked that we provide gazebos if it's raining,' reported Barbara.

'I'm amazed by this. I wouldn't have thought she'd want any tent pegs on her lawn.' Edna was well aware of Lorna's obsession with her lawn.

'Well, apparently she has allocated an area for us to use away from her main lawn as she doesn't want anyone to walk on that.'

Polly wondered what the point was in Lorna opening her garden if she was so paranoid about anyone walking on her lawn. After all, part of the enjoyment of viewing someone else's garden is to wander around.

'Lorna has also asked if we can take some teapots and cups and saucers with us as she's not sure if she will have enough to cater for everyone,' continued Barbara.

'How many people is she expecting?' asked Lizzy.

'About fifty, I think. How many tickets have you sold, Julia?' enquired Edna, hopeful that she might have some good news.

'Ten,' came the reply.

'Is that all?' shrieked Edna.

'Yes, and they're mostly committee members.'

'It hardly seems worth laying on a garden party for that few people. Has anyone told Lorna?' Edna wondered if she should call the whole thing off.

'Not yet. I thought we should wait and ring round. I'm

going to WI and my camera club next week so I'll try and sell some there,' Julia informed her.

'What a shame that our own members don't want to support an event like this,' observed Polly, aware that a lot of members had better things to do with their weekends. 'Maybe because it's on a Sunday. Perhaps our members want to spend the day with the family,' she suggested.

'Nevertheless, it is a poor show. Let's hope another club bails us out on this one as I don't relish the thought of telling Lorna that hardly anyone is coming.' Edna knew that Lorna was looking forward to it.

'Next item.' Edna tried to move the meeting on. 'How's our trip to Winchester coming along?'

'Fine,' said April. 'Everything's organised. We'll meet at the War Memorial at eight o'clock Friday morning. We should get back around six o'clock Saturday evening.'

'I'm really looking forward to it,' commented Polly.

'There's a craft fair on nearby that I thought we could go to on the Saturday morning, and then pop into a garden centre that afternoon where they're going to lay on a cream tea for us.'

'Sounds great. Can't wait,' muttered Sarah.

'Be good to get away for a couple of days. Though it sounds like the diet will be on hold for a bit longer.' That was nothing new for Polly. It didn't take much to steer her off course.

'What's happening about the stand at the supermarket?' enquired Edna.

'Everything's set up. We've got a desk in the foyer of the supermarket on the day after Winchester,' confirmed Rose.

'Why on earth are we doing it that day?' questioned

Edna, feeling slightly annoyed that Rose had gone ahead and finalised this without consulting her. She rolled her eyes. Even though she wasn't going to Winchester as she had other plans she had no intention of giving up her Sunday to help with the stand.

'That was the only day they could offer. I didn't like to turn them down after us putting pressure on them in the first place to allow us to sell flowers. Besides, they're giving us the flowers to sell and any money we make goes to our charity. I'll make some flower arrangements to sell, then on the day all we have to do is make hand-tied bouquets for anyone who buys the flowers.'

Polly smiled. She wasn't the fastest at making hand-tied bouquets at the best of times. 'Let's hope they've got lots of shopping to do so I have plenty of time to make them a bouquet,' she remarked.

Whenever she had to make a bouquet she would start by spiralling the stems. After a few flowers she would dismantle it as it clearly wasn't looking right. She'd start again, dismantle, start again, swear, dismantle and so on. In the end she did her best although often she wasn't totally impressed with it, but she knew that most people would think it was acceptable, it was just her desire to get things perfect that got in her way.

'I'm happy to do any hand-tied bouquets,' Rose offered, taking the pressure off Polly. After all she didn't want to have to run the stand on her own. She paused, trying to gauge Polly's reaction. 'Does this mean that you'll come along and help?' she continued.

Polly hadn't planned on giving up her Sunday, especially bearing in mind that she was away on the Friday and Saturday too, but she could sense that some of the other committee members weren't going to offer.

'Yes, that's fine,' she replied. 'It's only for the morning isn't it?'

'Absolutely. We set up at nine-thirty and we'll be gone by lunch-time, or when we sell all the flowers. Whichever is first.' Rose put Polly's mind at rest that she wasn't going to be there for the entire day.

'Count me in too,' chipped in Sarah. 'Sounds like fun.'

Rose looked round the table. 'Any more volunteers?' There were a couple of nods and April agreed to go if she wasn't too exhausted after organising the trip to Winchester.

'Unless there is anything else, I think we should conclude the meeting.' Edna was hoping to finish early this evening. She had been out all day and tiredness was starting to kick in.

'There is one thing,' said Rose. Edna looked at her in her usual authoritarian way over the top of her glasses. 'At our last club night I noticed Margery was a bit flustered and suddenly packed away a load of her plants. When I asked her if everything was OK she said to ask you, Edna.'

'Everything was fine. I just felt that a few of her plants shouldn't be sold. They are prone to causing skin irritation and I didn't want our members buying them,' she lied.

Polly looked at her and raised her eyebrows.

'Surely Margery would know that. After all she is a herbalist,' insisted Rose.

'Of sorts. She prescribes herbs but isn't a qualified herbalist,' stated Barbara as tactfully as she could, although she was aware that she sounded quite catty.

'I think she might have just made a mistake and brought along a few pots of plants that she shouldn't have. That's all.

No need to make a fuss over it.' Edna didn't want to get into a discussion about this.

'I'm not really. I was just concerned as our members love her plant sales and it seemed a shame to see her rushing off like that.'

'I'm sure everything will be fine at the next meeting. Don't worry about it.' Polly tried to reassure her, hoping that she would let the matter drop once and for all.

'One other thing before we end the meeting,' interrupted Edna, 'is that we should congratulate Polly and Sarah on their fantastic achievements at the show. Polly came first in her class and Sarah came second in hers.'

'Well done both of you. Polly, you must be so proud to finally get that first place.' Julia was genuinely enthusiastic. She rarely competed in any shows, and certainly not at the level Polly did so she was in awe of her success.

'I still can't believe it.'

'It looked fantastic,' complimented Lizzy.

'Sarah, your design was beautiful too. Had I been the judge I'd have given you first place,' stated Edna.

'The one that came first was lovely though.' Sarah defended the judges' choice.

'I think you were robbed. The first design looked oversized to me. I'm sure a leaf extended beyond the space allowed,' continued Edna, always quick to find fault if she didn't agree with the judges.

'Should've been disqualified then. After all, they disqualified Jennifer. Any idea why?' asked Julia, curious as to why the judges had done this.

'I think she might have used some endangered plant material,' Polly volunteered.

'What a shame. It doesn't exactly encourage people to enter shows, does it?' Julia had a point. It was often hard to get people to compete, and to be disqualified was hardly an incentive to spend the time and money on an exhibit.

A pang of guilt crossed Polly's mind. Perhaps she should have told Jennifer not to use the cannabis leaves in her design. But what's done was done and there was nothing she could do about it now.

FOURTEEN

ynthia felt slightly nervous about going to the show debrief meeting today. As she walked into the meeting doubts started to come into her mind over the incident with Polly and Amy. Had she made the right decision?

Diane opened the meeting. 'Generally I think the flower show was a tremendous success. We received some fabulous feedback and made a profit on the weekend, which is always a plus.'

The show committee looked pleased with themselves.

'There were a few incidents, however, that I think we need to review so that we can learn from them for future shows,' she continued. 'There were issues regarding Francesca's design, problems with the land exhibits and the incident regarding the exhibits falling over in the main marquee.'

Cynthia hadn't taken much notice of the other issues during the course of the weekend as she had been so caught up with the issue of Polly's exhibit collapsing, and was intrigued to hear what had happened.

Francesca had spent hours making some birds for her design. They were beautifully crafted and meticulously covered in seeds. They were definitely the crowning glory to her design. Fortunately the judges saw them at their best. The public weren't as lucky. A pigeon had been loitering near the marquee while the competitors were setting up their exhibits. On a number of occasions it had to be shooed out of the marquee as it was becoming a nuisance. It got its revenge by finding its way into the marquee once everyone had gone home and it spent the night devouring the seeds on the birds. By morning they had been pecked to shreds.

Added to the list of problems with the show, some squirrels had decided to mutilate several of the land art exhibits that had been set up outside the marquee. In many ways it was inevitable as nuts and other food were incorporated in them, but the squirrels clearly had a field day and by morning all that was left were random pieces of plant material. At least they had enjoyed the flower show!

'I don't think we could have done anything differently,' concluded Diane.

'Other than hired pest control to patrol the area,' suggested Vivienne.

'There's no way we can stop people using seeds or nuts in their exhibits, but perhaps we need to give out a warning in the schedule.'

'What, that their exhibit might be devoured by a pesky pigeon or greedy squirrel?' sniggered Hilary.

Cynthia wished she had seen this and had not been so caught up with the incident in the main marquee.

Diane laughed. 'I'll bear that in mind for next time. Now, the incident regarding the exhibits that fell over.'

Cynthia took a deep breath, wondering what Diane was going to say.

'Well done, Cynthia,' boomed Diane. 'You handled that difficult situation brilliantly.' Cynthia was surprised by the positive reaction but greatly relieved. 'Polly was adamant that Amy sabotaged her exhibit. What do you think?' asked Diane.

'I only arrived after the event, I'm afraid, so I can't say for sure.'

'I noticed Amy near her design once or twice when Polly wasn't there,' chipped in Vivienne, who had been setting up her design across the other side of the marquee but within sight of Amy.

'So do you think she had anything to do with it?' questioned Diane.

'I'd love to say she did as I can't stand the woman. We've had a few moments in the past when she stabbed me in the back. But in all honesty, I can't say for sure,' confessed Vivienne.

'Well, in the end sense prevailed. I think you did the right thing, Cynthia, and got the right result.'

'What about Amy's complaint?'

'Forget it. Judges' decision is final. If she's not happy, that's her problem.'

'Did you hear about the exhibitor who fell in the water trough?' asked Hilary.

'Is this a joke?' questioned Diane, not sure whether to take her seriously.

'No. Fact.'

There was laughter around the room.

'What happened?' asked Diane, who hadn't been privy to this story.

'Her floral foam fell to the bottom of the water trough while she was soaking it. She tried to retrieve it and fell in.'

Diane burst out laughing. 'Who was it? Anyone I know?'

'Denise Clark-Andrews.'

'Oh dear. I wondered why she gave me a filthy look when I saw her at the show and asked her how she'd got on.' She paused. 'On a serious note, I suppose we should make sure that we have a lower water trough at our next show, or ask people to bring their floral foam ready soaked.'

'We don't want our exhibitors drowning,' commented Hilary.

Vivienne made a note of this. 'I don't think we'll forget this in a hurry.'

'Well, it was a very interesting show. Let's hope the next show runs with a little less drama. I'm hoping we can count on your support again, Cynthia,' requested Diane.

Cynthia was taken aback by this question. She was thrilled to finally have been recognised and that at last she was able to put the past well and truly behind her. She left the meeting on a real high.

Amy was still seething. Malcolm had never seen her like this before and he was starting to get a bit worried. She ate very little at the best of times with her various fad diets, but since the show she was eating virtually nothing one minute and bingeing on anything 'naughty' the next. There were sweet wrappers, cake boxes and empty crisp packets in the bin, which took him by surprise.

'Everything all right, dear?' he dared to ask as she sat in the armchair; a packet of chocolate biscuits next to her.

'Fine,' she snapped.

'You can't carry on like this.'

'Like what?'

'Need you ask? I've never seen you like this before. You have to let this go or you'll make yourself ill.' Amy glared at Malcolm. 'Honestly, just let it go,' he reiterated, concern in his voice.

'That's easy for you to say. It's my reputation at stake here.'

'Well, I don't think your behaviour has done much to protect that. If you accepted defeat graciously people would think more highly of you.'

Amy thought back to the way she had behaved when she saw that Polly had beaten her, and that this was the first show she had come away from with nothing.

Malcolm could sense her thought process. 'Chalk this one down to experience and come back fighting at the next show,' he suggested.

Amy knew deep down that Malcolm was right. In her mind though, it wasn't quite as simple as that. She had built her reputation over years of competing and didn't feel comfortable to see someone else step in and take her crown. She was determined that she would regain her crown at the next show.

She looked beside her at the almost empty packet of chocolate biscuits. For a split second she had no memory of eating them and she wondered where they had gone.

Malcolm looked down at her and put his hand out. She handed him what was left of the packet. He looked disapprovingly at her when he saw that there were only a couple of biscuits left. 'I might as well finish off the packet then,' he responded as he headed to the kitchen to throw the wrapper away.

FIFTEEN

I t was a fairly ordinary day as far as Gillian was concerned. A few weeks had passed since the visit from the police about Robert and despite a few nightmares during that time, she had now settled back into her life.

She was doing a flower demonstration that evening and was busy getting her car loaded with all her containers and flowers as the police car drew up. Her heart raced as she saw the police heading in her direction. She stopped what she was doing and approached them.

Charles was in the house and noticed them arriving. He watched from the window and saw Gillian talking with them for some time. He was curious as to what they had said, but didn't want to get involved as the last time he commented on Robert's disappearance Gillian got upset and stormed off.

The police car drove off and Gillian went back to loading her car. Charles headed out of the house. 'What did they want?' he called out to Gillian. She was half in and half out of the car and, despite hearing him, she chose to ignore him. 'What did the police want?' he asked again.

She reluctantly put her head out of the car. 'Just to tell me that the DNA test has confirmed that it is Robert,' she said quite unemotionally, but deep inside she felt shocked.

'Oh,' replied Charles as he walked off, not wanting to engage in any further conversation with Gillian.

Gillian tried to hold the tears back. She could feel them welling up inside her but she was loath to let Charles see her cry. She tried to distract herself with sorting out her flowers for the evening demonstration but, no matter how hard she tried, she couldn't. On the one hand she felt relieved that there was no suggestion of foul play, so from that point of view she'd had a lucky escape. On the other hand, she knew she would have to telephone Robert's children and tell them that he had been found as she would need to make funeral arrangements for him. She decided to get it over and done with and headed indoors to make the phone call to Robert's children. Surprisingly the calls weren't as bad as she had expected and both seemed to accept what she said without too much discussion. However, she surmised that as soon as she put the phone down they would be in contact with each other to discuss what their next move was and how they could get their hands on Robert's estate.

Gillian tried to put this out of her mind. After all, she was due to set off for the flower demonstration and she didn't want anything to interfere with that. This was a new flower club she was visiting and, although she was going to repeat the same demonstration that she had done at other clubs all year round, she didn't want to feel unnerved by today's happenings.

She put her head around the front door and called out to Charles. 'Bye. See you later.' He grunted a response of some sort and she headed off to find somewhere quiet where she could think about what had happened.

Margery arrived at the crematorium fairly early. She couldn't remember the exact time Gillian had said the funeral would take place and she didn't want to take any chances by being late. She was surprised at how many other people were already there. She walked past them, acknowledging them, although she didn't recognise anyone. It was only when she was about to enter the chapel that she realised that she was at the wrong funeral. Panic hit her and she made a quick exit just as the hearse was pulling in.

When she saw all the flowers in the hearse she realised she had definitely gate-crashed someone else's funeral as the flowers were all for a woman, and definitely not Robert. She smiled to herself. She was glad she had realised her mistake before she made a complete fool of herself.

She decided to have a walk round the grounds while she waited. They were particularly beautiful and peaceful. She hadn't been to the crematorium since Henry's funeral and, before that, Duncan's so it always brought back a lot of painful memories for her.

She watched people from the earlier funeral leaving the chapel and it wasn't long before Gillian arrived with Charles in the funeral procession. Robert's children were in the second car in the cortege. They had changed a lot since she had last seen them, which was hardly surprising as they rarely visited Robert and, when they did, it was invariably because they wanted something from him.

Gillian got out of the car and waited for Charles to walk round to stand at her side. They stood in silence as Robert's coffin was carried out of the hearse and taken into the chapel. She was relieved that the coffin spray that she had made for it looked quite stunning. She had decided to keep the design fairly conservative with just red roses and foliage which she thought he would like. It had taken her a couple of hours to make as she wanted it to be perfect. It was only spoilt by the fact that Robert's children decided to send a rather garish funeral tribute that had also been placed in the hearse next to his coffin.

As they walked into the chapel Gillian acknowledged Margery sitting towards the back of the room and was relieved to at least have one friendly face there.

Gillian didn't say a word throughout the whole service. Both of his children decided to say something about their father, and a long-time friend of Robert's read from the Bible. Gillian felt slightly overcome with emotion. Not only because of Robert, but the last time she had been in this chapel was at Henry's funeral. Memories of her life with Henry came flooding back to her and she found herself with tears streaming down her face. Charles gave her a sideways glance and put his hand on her arm to give her some reassurance. He was unaware that she was crying for Henry and not for Robert.

The service went by in a blur and it wasn't long before Gillian was standing outside thanking all the well-wishers for attending. Robert's children came and stood by her. For a split second she thought she saw some hint of kindness in their eyes.

'What are you going to do now, Gillian?' asked Robert's daughter, Fran.

'Carry on as normal, I guess. At least we now know what happened.'

'Do you think you'll stay in the house or sell it?' Gillian wasn't surprised by the question.

'This has all been a shock. I'm not sure yet what I'm going to do.' Fran seemed satisfied with the answer for now. 'Are you coming back to the house for some refreshments?' Gillian offered.

Fran nodded and they both agreed to head back with her. Gillian hoped she hadn't made a mistake inviting them. They hadn't set foot inside the house since Robert's disappearance and she certainly didn't want them making trouble for her. She just hoped that Charles kept a low profile and didn't say anything that was likely to upset them. Charles had nothing nice to say about Robert, despite the fact that he had been living in his house for the past couple of years.

Fortunately Gillian's fears were totally unfounded. If they were checking out the house and what their inheritance was likely to be at some point they didn't show it. She offered them some of Robert's personal belongings which they seemed pleased with.

Margery headed over to where Gillian was. 'Have they said anything about the house?' she asked, curiosity getting the better of her.

'They asked if I was going to sell it. After all, now that we know Robert's dead there's not much they can do until either I decide to move or I die.'

'True. Have the police said any more about his death?'

Gillian felt a shiver run through her. She had tried to block everything from her mind about that fateful cruise, and the last thing she wanted was Margery reminding her of what she had done. 'No, they haven't. As far as I'm concerned the matter is now closed,' replied Gillian, somewhat coldly.

Margery took the hint and let out a sigh of relief that perhaps this matter had now gone away.

SIXTEEN

pril was standing beside the layby when Polly and Sarah arrived. 'Thanks for coming on time,' she said as she ticked them off on her list. 'The coach should be here soon.' A large group of women had already congregated with a variety of suitcases. Polly looked over and noticed Jennifer struggling with her bag. 'Need a hand?' she offered, although somewhat surprised by the size of the case as they were only going away for one night.

'Thank you. I thought your flower arrangement at the show was lovely,' she said. Polly was still on cloud nine after coming first and was more than happy to have people compliment her.

'How did you get on, Jennifer?' Although Polly already knew the answer she didn't want to let Jennifer know that.

'The judges didn't like it. They questioned my use of some of my plant material, saying that it was banned, but I don't understand that. They wrote "NAS" on my card. What does that mean?'

'It means Not According to Schedule.' Polly thought the decision was a little harsh. She didn't feel she could tell her the reason, otherwise Jennifer might wonder why Polly hadn't warned her when she popped along and saw her design. 'What a shame. It's surprising what is on the list of forbidden materials. For example, you're not allowed to use coral or endangered plants, so maybe you had something like that,' she added, trying to convince Jennifer.

'Maybe.'

'At least you were happy with it. After all, that's what really matters, isn't it?' She felt her answer was somewhat patronising but Jennifer seemed pleased with it.

The coach pulled in, which was a relief for Polly as it gave her an excuse to escape the conversation.

'Mind if I go in the front?' she asked April before anyone else could get to the coach door. 'You know how travel-sick I get.'

'That's fine. I've reserved the front seat for you anyway.'

Sarah and Polly took up their seats at the front of the coach behind the driver while everyone else made their way to their seats. As usual one person was late and on this occasion it was Belinda. She seemed to live on a different timeframe from everyone else. She rarely wore a watch and when she did it was invariably wrong. Eventually she arrived, slightly frazzled at having to rush to get there before the coach left.

When the coach finally got going Polly wondered if she had made a mistake by grabbing the front seat. She was sitting so high up that when Bob, the coach driver, lowered the sunblind, all she could see was the road before her which was making her feel slightly queasy.

'You OK?' asked Sarah, noticing that Polly was starting to look a bit pale and well aware of Polly's difficulty of travelling on a coach.

'Hopefully. Just wish I could see out the front window.'

'Look out the side window.'

'I'll be OK.' Polly wasn't totally sure.

Vertigo plagued her and she knew exactly what she needed to avoid in order to prevent an attack. Seeing the countryside whizzing past her was definitely a trigger and she didn't want her weekend ruined by it. In many ways Polly had learned to live with her condition, although sometimes it got the better of her. She had lost count of the number of times she had broken a toe as she stumbled across a room into a doorway when an attack came upon her from out of the blue. She even had an old pair of walking boots that she had held on to purely to wear on occasions of a toe fracture, as they were the only things she could ever get on her feet. Not that these boots came without risk. On one occasion she went to get up from her chair and one set of lace hooks had got caught up with the laces on the other boot and she ended up flying across the room into a door. Another time, the extremely long bootlace got trapped under the wheels of the chair she was sitting on. When she got up she found herself towing the chair behind her. This might have been funny except for the fact that she was at an interview at the time and it didn't exactly instil confidence in her prospective employer. She didn't know if this was why she didn't get the job, although the fact that she arrived late and windswept, wearing an old pair of walking boots with her suit, probably didn't help her case.

She took a sweet out of her handbag. Perhaps this would distract her attention. It seemed to work for a while.

'Do you want to have a short stop?' Bob asked over his shoulder.

'Yes please,' replied Polly before April had a chance to get a word in.

'There's a service station a few miles away. I'll pull off the motorway there.'

Polly felt relieved that they were going to stop, least of all because she was gasping for a cup of tea. She hadn't risked drinking anything before setting off that morning, just in case there were no facilities on the coach.

The coach slowly made its way down to the coach park.

'Looks busy,' commented Polly, seeing all the coaches already parked up.

As the coach came to a standstill April stood up. 'Ladies, can you all be back here by ten o'clock.'

Polly and Sarah were first off the coach. There was a slight chill in the air but the blue sky suggested it could turn into a beautiful day.

When everyone had got off the coach they headed in a crocodile line to the service station, all popped into the ladies room, then went into one of the many restaurants to grab a cup of tea or coffee. The service station was nothing special. It could have been anywhere, with overpriced food and drink served in polystyrene containers, but at least it was something.

Polly and Sarah sat down with their drinks. 'Tell me some more about this bloke you're meeting.' Polly was curious as always.

'Don't.'

'Don't what?'

'I feel really nervous about it and I'm trying not to think about it.'

'It's only a blind date.'

'Yes, but I've got high hopes this time and I'm worried either I'll be disappointed or he won't like me.'

'Nonsense. It'll be fine.' Polly tried to reassure her although she was glad she was in a relationship and didn't have to go through this whole courting ritual again.

'He sounds great. His emails are extremely well-written and very sensitive.'

'Sounds all right to me. You never know, perhaps he's the one.' Polly tried to instil confidence in Sarah.

'We'll see.' Sarah glanced at her watch. 'Suppose we'd better get going.'

Polly discarded what was left of her tea. The teabags used at this service station were very strong and, despite removing the tea bag as quickly as possible, the tea tasted very bitter.

They walked back to the coach. April was already there counting everyone back as they took their seats. 'Just one more person,' she informed Bob, who was starting to get agitated as he was aware that the roads were getting busy and he didn't relish being stuck in a traffic jam for hours.

'Who's missing?' asked Sarah.

'Belinda.'

'I might have guessed,' sighed Polly.

'I'll go and have another look round the service station just to be sure.' Sarah got off the coach. 'Don't go without me,' she joked.

Sarah did a quick circuit of the service station and returned a few minutes later. 'No sign of her I'm afraid.'

'How strange. Where on earth can she be? Has anyone seen Belinda?' April asked the rest of the ladies on the coach. They shrugged their shoulders.

Polly looked out of the side window, gazing at the coach that was parked next to them. 'She's over there,' she shouted.

All heads turned to the coach next to theirs. Sitting quite comfortably and looking at them was Belinda. She looked slightly confused when she saw the familiar faces staring back at her and then a look of panic appeared on her face as she realised she was sitting on the wrong coach. She quickly got up and gathered up her belongings, pushed her way past the bemused ladies and got off. She looked extremely embarrassed as she got back on the correct coach. Everyone started to cheer and clap which made her blush even more.

'I'm so sorry. I was sure that was our coach.'

'Didn't you notice that there was no one you knew?' enquired April, surprised that Belinda was totally unaware that she was sitting on the wrong coach.

'Not really. I was the first one on it and didn't pay much attention to the other people when they arrived. Although I must admit that I thought it was strange that Joan and Freda weren't sitting opposite me.'

'You must have got a real surprise when you saw us looking at you,' said Polly, trying to stifle her laughter.

'For a second it didn't register, then I realised what had happened. Thank God I did, otherwise I could have ended up anywhere.'

'It wouldn't have been that bad. I gather that coach is heading to the flower show too so you would at least have arrived at the correct destination,' replied Bob, who had been chatting to the other coach driver while the ladies were having their comfort stop.

Belinda settled back into her seat and the chatter on the coach subsided slightly as the coach set off for the final part of the journey. After the incident at the service station, the rest of the journey was straightforward and they made good time.

'I'll be back to pick you up at five, ladies. Then we'll head to the hotel,' Bob told them as he pulled into a layby a short walk from the flower festival. 'I don't think I can get any closer than this, I'm afraid.'

As Belinda got off the coach Bob stopped her. 'Please remember which coach you've got to catch next time. I'd hate to see you end up in the wrong place.'

Polly and Sarah laughed but Belinda didn't see the funny side of it. The joke was definitely wearing very thin by then and she wished she could just forget about it and enjoy the rest of the trip.

The sun was already shining brightly and the temperature had gone up several degrees since they left home. Polly removed the cardigan she was wearing and tied it round her waist. 'Cor, might even get a suntan,' she said.

'Yeah, that sun is hot,' observed Sarah.

They followed a constant trail of ladies who were clearly heading to the flower festival.

Polly laughed. 'Funny how you can tell a flower arranger a mile off. There seems to be something very distinctive about them.'

'What, ladies of a certain age carrying lots of shopping bags?'

'Exactly.'

As they approached the cathedral where the festival was taking place they noticed some interesting hanging designs round the outside of the building, inviting people into the cathedral. The queue to get in was relatively short, despite the number of people milling around. Some were obviously more interested in grabbing a cup of coffee or heading round the many gardening stalls that had been set up in the grounds of the cathedral.

'Cuppa or festival?' asked Polly, always happy to stop for a cup of tea and a piece of cake.

'Let's go into the festival before it gets full. It'll be heaving later.'

Polly knew it made perfect sense to do this, but was a little disappointed at not visiting the nearby tea room.

The show was up to its usual standard with spectacular displays around the entrance hall. Polly and Sarah made their way inside, following the line of ladies in front of them.

'Wow, look at that.' Polly pointed to a large design of orchids suspended from the ceiling and overhanging a pool of water with a mirror base. 'I wonder how they did that.' She scrutinised the mechanics. Her brain was already processing the data in case she decided to do something similar at a forthcoming show.

'Don't tell me you're planning your next design already.'

'Well, I love it. Look at the fantastic reflection in the water. Umm...' Polly was miles away as she tried to visualise how this would look in one of her creations. She delved round in her oversized handbag for her phone so that she could take a few photos of it in case her memory failed her.

'Don't look now.' Sarah interrupted her thoughts.

'What?'

'Your friend is over there.'

Polly glanced in between a group of ladies and an urn overflowing with roses. Standing still and looking at one of the designs was Amy.

'Oh my God. Can't I go anywhere without the risk of bumping into her again?' Polly ducked down not wanting to be seen by her.

'You've done nothing wrong. She's the one who should feel awkward, not you,' insisted Sarah.

'I know but I'm not in the mood for confrontation this weekend. I'm here to enjoy myself.'

Polly kept a close eye on her. She wasn't sure if Amy had seen her or not. 'Why don't we go and get a cuppa and something to eat now. We can come back later.'

'Good idea.'

They pushed their way past a group of ladies and spotted an exit, which they made a beeline for. Once outside Polly felt relieved. 'That was a close shave.'

'Let's head into the town centre and find a café where we can get some lunch,' suggested Sarah, pleased that her keen observation had averted a difficult situation.

By then the town centre was extremely busy with a selection of market stalls set up on the pavement. They headed towards the end of the High Street and discovered a café that was relatively quiet. They chose a table near the window. Polly put her cardigan on the back of the chair. She hooked the straps of her handbag over her knees, something she always did when she sat in a café. She was paranoid about getting her handbag snatched. This had happened to her once before when a small child crawled under the seat and took her bag. Fortunately, the police found the abandoned bag in a rubbish bin a few blocks away. All her money was gone, but at least she still had her bag which had been a present from Mark. After that experience she didn't want to take any chances.

She opened up the menu. The choice of food was fairly limited so she ordered her usual jacket potato with baked beans and melted cheese. Sarah, who had a variety of special dietary requirements, discussed options with the waiter until they had concocted a somewhat strange combination of food between them.

Polly looked out of the window, engrossed in a drama that was unfolding a few feet away from the café on the pavement.

'What are you looking at?' asked Sarah as she handed the menu back to the waiter.

'They've just come along and watered the hanging baskets. That man stood under one of them and has got soaked.'

Sarah looked out of the window at all the commotion. There was a lot of shouting going on as the man yelled abuse at the person who had just watered the basket.

'Never a dull moment, eh?'

'Not when we're around,' Sarah laughed, aware that they invariably attracted rather funny or odd situations.

'So, what are you wearing for your date?' Polly changed the subject.

'Not sure. I suspect I'll chop and change my mind.' Sarah hadn't given this much thought yet, although the date was fast approaching.

'Go for something casual. You look good in that new blue shirt of yours.' Polly tried to be helpful.

'Maybe you're right. Not sure what impression I want to make.'

'Hopefully the right one.' Polly smiled. She knew that Sarah was terrified about going and was likely to be extremely stressed by the time the day arrived.

The café was fast filling up. Sarah glanced round the room. 'Looks like we timed this just right.' She watched as some new arrivals were shown to their table. Their waiter was running round in all directions and they were relieved to see him finally heading towards their table with their lunch.

Polly looked over at Sarah's plate. 'That looks interesting,' she said, curious as to the mixture of foods.

Sarah seemed quite pleased with her choice of dishes. 'Well, at least this will fill a gap until we stop for tea and cake later.' Sarah had no doubt that they would sniff out some home-made cake at some stage.

They didn't waste any time in devouring their lunch. The noise in the café got louder and louder as more people arrived. Polly looked at her watch. 'Shall we go back to the show now?' she asked, aware that time was moving on and they still had a lot to see before they got back on the coach.

Sarah nodded. Her expression suddenly changed. 'You'll never guess who's sitting at the table over there.'

Polly looked over and saw Amy and Malcolm reading the menu. 'It's like she's following me around.'

'Quick, pay the bill and let's go,' suggested Sarah, not wanting a scene and knowing how Polly felt about her.

Polly put some money down on the silver plate on the table and headed for the door. But it was too late. Amy had spotted Polly. It didn't help that Polly dropped her cardigan on the floor as she was walking out of the café and was called back by the waiter to collect it.

'Hello,' said Amy.

'Hello,' Polly replied, trying to be polite and hoping that Amy didn't want to engage in conversation. She started to walk away. As far as she was concerned all the niceties were over.

'I'm sorry,' Amy called after her. Polly turned around and headed back in Amy's direction.

'What for?'

'What happened.'

'So you did sabotage my design?'

'No, I said I didn't. I'm sorry about my behaviour.'

'Oh, that.' Polly was disappointed she had not received a confession.

'I shouldn't have behaved that way. I was just upset.' Polly got the feeling Amy had to force the words out. It was clear that an apology hadn't come naturally to her and she suspected Malcolm had something to do with this gesture.

'That's OK, no problem,' Polly lied. She still thought Amy had been the reason why her design had toppled and she had been totally unimpressed by her behaviour, but she didn't want to get into a full scale discussion.

'I think stress gets to us all sometimes,' chipped in Sarah. 'Come on, Polly, we need to get going.' She tried to hurry her along.

Sarah's intervention seemed to work and they both headed out of the restaurant into the pedestrianised shopping area without turning back to see if Amy was watching them.

'Thanks for that.'

'For what?'

'Getting me out of there.'

'Well, at least she's apologised.'

'Yes, but she won't admit she tampered with my stand though, will she?'

'Maybe she didn't. Maybe it just got damaged somewhere along the way.'

Polly hadn't even thought about this, so convinced that

Amy was to blame. She recalled the commotion with the journey there, having to load the stand, then unload it and then reload it back in the car after the puncture. Who knew if it got damaged, but it was possible that something had weakened that part of the stand.

'What's done is done. Fact is, I won anyway,' she said smugly, not wanting to think that Amy wasn't to blame after all.

'Exactly.'

Polly looked at her surroundings. A brightly coloured t-shirt caught her eye on one of the market stalls. 'That's perfect,' she said over her shoulder as she made a beeline for it.

'You'll look good in that,' confirmed Sarah.

'Not for me, for you,' Polly replied. 'I thought you could wear this on your date.'

Sarah cringed. Her taste in clothes was very different from Polly's. Polly loved bright colours, but Sarah always erred on the side of caution and took a much more conservative approach to her choice of clothes.

'Why don't you get it?' suggested Sarah, believing full well that it would suit Polly.

'I might just do that,' replied Polly. 'Although I'll have to sneak it in the house as I've promised Mark I'll cut back on my spending.' Before Sarah could reply Polly had pulled her purse out and was paying the stall keeper.

'Well, you didn't take much convincing.'

Polly smiled. 'I just had to have it.'

They headed back to the festival for a proper look around before Polly found anything else she could buy, although it wasn't long before she had discovered some garden ornaments for sale on one of the stalls that she just had to have.

'Think I need a hand getting these back to the coach,' she said as she tried to pick up the various ornaments she had selected. 'Can you carry the duck, and I'll take the giant flower and the dung beetle?' she asked Sarah.

Sarah was laughing. 'Who on earth has a metal dung beetle in their garden?'

'That's the point. Not many people!' Polly smiled. 'I'll tell Mark I bought it for him. I think he'll see the funny side of this.'

Laden with all Polly's purchases, they headed back to the coach.

Bob's face dropped when he saw the group of women waiting for him at the agreed spot. They were surrounded by bags, stands, vases and branches of wood.

April could sense there was a problem. 'Welcome to the world of flowers,' she said to him.

'When you said you'd have a lot of things to go on the coach, I thought you were talking about suitcases, not all this stuff.'

'Now you know why I insisted we booked the larger coach with more boot space. You've obviously never been on a trip with flower arrangers before.'

'No.'

'Well, this is pretty normal for us. Just wait until tomorrow.'

'Why?'

'I doubt anyone will come back from the craft show or garden centre empty-handed. I suspect we'll be buying loads of plants and other things.' She relished in the idea of finding that 'must have' item.

'I don't think we've got enough room for all this stuff.'

'We'll have to make room one way or another. There's no

way I'm going to tell these ladies they can't buy any more goodies tomorrow.'

Bob certainly didn't feel that he could either. He would have to repack the coach carefully the following morning after breakfast.

Once Bob had loaded all the 'stuff' onto the coach he set off. There were no stragglers this time. Even Belinda had managed to arrive on time. It was a relatively short drive before the coach turned off the main road and headed down a country lane. There was only one building in the distance and they seemed to be heading for that. The coach started to slow down and drove over a cattle grid as it entered the long driveway to the hotel.

'Is this where we're staying?' Sarah asked.

'Yes. It's a stately home,' answered April.

'Very posh.' Polly wasn't expecting this for the amount of money they had been charged for their stay. 'I can't believe how reasonable it is.'

'You know April. She's always good at getting deals for us,' acknowledged Sarah, aware of the fact that April was always after a bargain, whether it was a new outfit from the charity shop or some goods from the boot sale. April wasn't the sort of person to pay full price for anything. Even the flowers she would buy for her flower arrangements were reduced price ones that she bought from the supermarket. Rarely they lasted more than a day or two.

'Ladies. When you've checked in can everyone meet in the bar at seven o'clock for pre-dinner drinks?' she called out as everyone started to leave the coach and unload their cases.

Check-in was relatively painless and Polly was given

the entry card to her room which was on the first floor. She climbed the stairs rather than wait for the lift with the others and located her room. It was an extremely grand affair with a huge bed in the centre and an armchair to the side looking out of the window. The views across the countryside were quite spectacular.

She lay down on the bed and gazed at the ceiling. It was extremely high with ornate coving. She could hear the floorboards creaking as whoever occupied the room above her walked around.

She was feeling quite peckish as lunch seemed a long time ago. They never did track down a tea room with home-made cakes. Polly got too carried away with shopping and the time just seemed to vanish. She reached into her bag for a packet of biscuits she had brought along 'in case of emergency.' Most had already been eaten and what was left was crushed. She poured a handful of crumbs into her hand and threw them into her mouth. Half hit their target, but half ended up across her face and in her hair. She laughed.

'I don't believe it,' she muttered to herself as she wiped her face.

There was just about enough time for a quick wash-and-brush-up before heading to the bar for the pre-dinner drinks that April had arranged to be served before everyone went into the dining-room.

Polly could hear the loud chattering well before she reached the bar. The flower show was very much the main topic of conversation. As she entered the room Jennifer headed straight for her.

'When's your next show, Polly?' asked Jennifer, curious to see if she could pick up any tips.

'Not for a few months. It's a tough one as it's an all-nighter,' she replied.

'What do you mean?'

'We don't start setting up until 10 p.m., and run through until 6 a.m. the following day.'

Jennifer was impressed. 'Don't think I'd be any good at that. I like to go to bed early.'

'It is very hard, but adrenaline carries you through the night. It's the next day I always feel so ill as I'm exhausted.'

'What are you doing for it?'

'Haven't decided yet. Wanted to get the area show out of the way first, now I can concentrate on this next show. The title of the class is "Serendipity".' Polly's stomach churned at the realisation that time was starting to run out and she hadn't come up with a design yet. She would need to put her thinking-cap on fairly rapidly, especially after her recent success she felt the pressure building on her to do well at the show.

Sarah came and stood beside Polly and touched her hair. Polly looked at her. 'Any reason why you've got a biscuit crumb in your hair?' Sarah asked as she removed the offending item.

'Saving it for later in case I get a bit peckish,' Polly replied before turning back to the conversation with Jennifer.

'Shall we get some drinks?' asked Polly.

There was a queue at the bar and by the time Polly returned with their drinks, April was already ordering everyone into the dining-room. In complete contrast to the rest of the hotel the restaurant had a more contemporary décor.

'Very nice,' Sarah commented as she saw the way the room had been set out. 'Though I'm not sure about those flowers.' She pointed to the design in the fireplace.

Polly glanced over at it. She smiled. 'No, the balance is all wrong. If they moved those peonies into the centre more, and the carnations towards the edge, it would look much better.'

April overheard her. 'Trust you to be critical. Now that you're a first-prize winner.'

Polly laughed. 'There have to be some perks from winning that.'

The waitress arrived with the food. It looked beautiful but the portions were tiny.

Polly's heart sank. It had been a long time since lunch and she was starving, especially as they never did get the promised piece of cake that afternoon.

Sarah sensed her frustration. 'Well, it is fine dining.'

'Why do they think you don't want to eat much just because it's posh food?' asked Polly, in dismay.

'Suppose it wouldn't look as stunning if it was a plateful,' reasoned Sarah.

Polly looked at the three pieces of ravioli sitting in the centre of a huge bowl. She picked up one of the pieces. It was delicious. She just wished she had a plateful rather than the frugal portion that had been placed before her.

'It's lovely, isn't it?' asked Sarah, who for once had managed to find something on the menu she could eat without needing to negotiate.

'Not wanting to spoil your meal, but did you see Amy today?' asked Lizzy.

Polly pulled a face. 'That woman seems to be following us around. Couldn't get away from her.'

'Tell Lizzy about the "apology",' suggested Sarah.

'What? She apologised for sabotaging your design?' Lizzy was intrigued.

'No. She apologised for behaving the way she did. She still insists she had nothing to do with my exhibit falling over.'

'A likely story.' As far as Lizzy was concerned Amy was as guilty as hell, or at least that was the rumour she was spreading.

The waitress returned to clear their plates, which were all pretty much licked clean. She returned a few minutes later with the main course. She put a very large plate down in front of Polly. In the centre was a tiny portion of fish on a bed of something unrecognisable. She started to walk away.

'Excuse me.' Polly caught her attention. 'Are there any vegetables to go with this?'

'No, madam.' The waitress walked off.

'Well, you can't say fairer than that,' said Lizzy, laughing.

Polly devoured her miniscule portion and looked longingly at Sarah's plate of pasta in a vegetable sauce. For once she wished she'd ordered the same as Sarah, who seemed to get a huge portion by comparison.

'Want some of mine?' Sarah asked her, well aware that Polly was pretty much drooling over her plate of food.

'Only if you don't want it.' Polly knew she was a walking dustbin and her constant battle with her weight was probably a result of this.

Sarah passed Polly her plate. 'Enjoy.'

Polly's eyes lit up and she sat silently as she finished off Sarah's meal. She looked up. Lizzy and Sarah were watching her and laughing.

'It would be a terrible waste not to eat it,' Polly said to justify her actions as the waitress cleared away the plate, curious as to why Polly had two in front of her.

The dessert arrived.

'Now that's more like it,' thought Polly as the waitress placed a dish with an oversized portion of banoffee pavlova on the table in front of her.

Sarah looked at the plate she had been given. She had a considerably smaller portion than Polly. 'Looks like you're getting preferential treatment.'

'Or she's realised that I'm a pig,' replied Polly as she tucked into the very rich dessert. She was loath to admit it but this was even too much for her. Somehow she managed to force in every mouthful despite starting to feel quite sick.

'Would you like to take your coffee in the lounge?' asked the waitress, keen to get the tables cleared so she could have a reasonably early night.

'How civilised,' commented Lizzy to April as all the ladies headed into the lounge.

'It's wonderful here, isn't it?' April was clearly pleased with herself for booking this hotel and relieved that it had lived up to her expectations.

Coffee arrived and was drunk and the ladies started to head off after their tiring day walking round the festival.

'I'm heading to bed. See you in the morning.' Polly felt quite drained. She was also aware that her pavlova was lying considerably heavy in her stomach and she decided she was in no mood for socialising. As soon as she got into her bedroom she rummaged through her washbag with some desperation in the hope of locating some indigestion tablets. Although they were rather crushed and past their 'use by' date she thought that this was better than nothing.

She got into bed and propped herself up with the pillows. Lying flat was not an option, feeling the way she did. After a short time she drifted off into a very uneasy sleep and vivid dream. The pavlova appeared as some life form that followed her round. No matter how much she ate it got larger and larger. She tried running away from it, but everywhere she turned it seemed to be.

She awoke with a start and looked around the bedroom. She was relieved there was no sign of the pavlova. The indigestion tablets seemed to have done their job and she felt a lot better but sleep wouldn't return. She got up again and this time located a herbal sleeping pill she kept for emergencies, along with some foam earplugs. It was still quite early and clearly whoever was occupying the room above hadn't gone to sleep yet.

Polly hadn't worked out who was in that room, but whoever it was they trudged around like a herd of elephants. The noise of the creaking floorboards was beginning to get on her nerves. She took the sleeping pill and put the earplugs in and settled down in the hope of getting to sleep again.

SEVENTEEN

Polly was awoken abruptly by the sound of the alarm on her phone. She wasn't used to hearing that and it made her jump. Her earplugs had fallen out in the night and were on the pillow beside her. She thought back to the strange dream she'd had and smiled.

Despite gorging herself the night before she was feeling ravenous, so she quickly got out of bed, showered and dressed. She packed her bag ready for the next part of the coach journey and headed down to the dining-room for breakfast. She was greeted at the doorway by a different waitress from the one she had seen the evening before. Spotting Sarah sitting at the table they had occupied at dinner, she headed in her direction.

'What are you laughing about?' Polly was curious.

'There's a chap over there in the corner. Don't look.'

Polly immediately turned round. Sarah tutted. 'I said, don't look!'

'What about him?'

'He's trying to impress the people he's with. They were

commenting on the wrapper on the cheese they've chosen for breakfast. He told them that the red outside was a natural rind on the cheese.'

'What, the wax coating?'

'Exactly.'

Polly started sniggering. 'You're joking!'

'No. He even called the waiter over to ask him.'

'What did he say?'

'He looked at him as though he was mad.'

'I don't believe it. Well, you get all sorts don't you?'

'I think we're definitely staying in a nuthouse.'

'Why?'

'When you arrived, did the waitress say anything to you about your room number?'

'Yes – I told her it was twenty-one and she said that she had been twenty-one once,' observed Polly.

'When I told her that my room was twenty-two she said she had been twenty-two once. In fact, everyone who has arrived for breakfast has been greeted with the same comment.'

They both watched as Lizzy entered the restaurant.

'Can I have your room number please?' asked the waitress.

'Twenty-six.'

'That's a nice number. I was twenty-six once,' said the waitress.

Polly and Sarah burst out laughing. 'See, what did I tell you?'

Lizzy looked over at their table, wondering what was so funny. 'Trust you two to be up to no good as usual.' Lizzy sat down at the table. She looked over at Sarah's plate of food. 'Hungry, are we?' she asked.

Sarah had decided to take full advantage of the breakfast buffet and pretty much try everything that was available, or at least what she could eat with all her special dietary requirements. 'I might as well,' she replied. 'At home, most days I can't even be bothered with a bowl of cereal.'

'Let's go and get ours,' Polly suggested to Lizzy, excited that there was definitely no fine dining at this meal. They both headed to the breakfast bar and proceeded to load up a tray with food. They returned some time later with enough food to feed a small army.

'At least we won't need to buy lunch today,' observed Lizzy, although in reality they probably would still do that.

They forced the food down. Despite being well and truly full up after the eggs on toast, Polly couldn't resist a couple of the mini pastries too. She had one on her plate that she just couldn't manage, so she discreetly put her napkin on her lap and slipped it into that. She then put it in her handbag.

Sarah watched her with amazement. 'Did I just see you pinching a pastry?'

'Yes. Well, I'm not exactly pinching it. We've paid for this so I'm taking it to have as my elevenses just in case I get a bit peckish.'

'What a good idea.' Lizzy headed back to the buffet table and returned a few seconds later with a couple of pastries on her plate before trying to secrete them in her handbag.

'You two are hopeless,' said Sarah, laughing.

'You'll regret it if you haven't got anything to eat later,' commented Lizzy, trying to defend her actions.

'OK, OK, I'll go and get one too,' and she headed off to load up her handbag.

Fully-fed and with handbags bulging, they headed back

to their rooms to collect their cases before checking out of the hotel.

Bob was already at the coach, desperately trying to repack everything with all the additional items that were purchased yesterday. He loaded all the suitcases and did a lot of groaning and tutting as he was doing this.

'What's his problem?' asked Polly, rather concerned that he didn't look too happy.

'He didn't realise that we like to buy lots of things when we're away,' answered April, still feeling rather annoyed that he had arrived with a coach without a large storage space, despite her requests for plenty of boot space. She got on to the coach to do a quick head-count. 'Just a couple yet to come.' Once again Belinda was missing. She started to laugh. 'Let's hope she hasn't got on another coach, otherwise she could end up anywhere today.'

'I'm pretty sure I saw her in the lobby,' assured Polly.

Belinda rushed out to the coach, or at least as fast as she could with the weight of her suitcase having made several large purchases the day before. 'Hope I'm not holding everyone up.'

'No problem, you're not the last,' reassured April.

The final person arrived shortly afterwards and, much to Bob's relief, he was able to fit all the cases into the coach storage space and still have a small amount of room left for any other things that were purchased today.

April picked up the microphone. A high-pitched squeak from the speaker alerted all the ladies on the coach that she wanted to make an announcement. 'Let's get going. Ladies, I hope you all enjoyed your stay.'

There was a general mumbling of approval.

'Today we're heading over to visit a craft fair where they have a special exhibition of mosaics on at the moment. We'll have lunch there before we head to a garden centre where they are serving us cream teas before we head for home. Journey time this morning is about forty-five minutes,' she continued. She sat down, pleased that the trip was going extremely well so far, despite the slight mix-up with Belinda.

Polly was feeling a bit better today, knowing that it was a relatively short ride to their first destination.

'What are you smirking about?' asked Sarah, who noticed a grin on Polly's face.

'I was just thinking about the time we went to the flower show in Blackpool and the cock-up with the hotels.'

A smiled filled Sarah's face as she recalled the mix-up with hotels. They didn't know that there were two hotels with the same name. In many ways this was a disaster waiting to happen.

'You need to book into the Brown Hotel,' Polly had instructed Lizzy and Maggie, who were also planning going there.

As there was no organised coach trip to the show everyone was making their way by train. Having already taken most of her annual leave, Polly couldn't get to the show until late that week, so she and Sarah booked trains for the Friday. Maggie and Lizzy had decided to go a couple of days earlier, with the idea that they would all meet up in the hotel lobby on the Friday evening when Polly and Sarah arrived, so that they could have dinner together. Polly then went on-line and booked rooms for herself and Sarah. Lizzy also went on-line and booked her and Maggie's rooms.

Everything seemed to be going smoothly and the journey from London was far quicker and easier than they had expected. When Polly and Sarah arrived in Blackpool, they walked the short distance to the hotel and got changed. It wasn't in a particularly nice part of town. The view from the window on one side was a strip club and on the other side a sex shop, but at least the hotel was central enough for the show.

The agreed meeting time was 7 p.m. that evening so Polly and Sarah sat in the hotel lobby waiting for Maggie and Lizzy to arrive. At 7.30 p.m. there was still no sign of them.

'Perhaps I got the time wrong,' confessed Polly. 'I'm sure we said seven, but maybe it was seven-thirty.'

They waited and waited and still there was no sign of Maggie and Lizzy. 'Have you got Maggie's number, Sarah? I've left my phone in my room.' Sarah dialled it and reached Maggie almost immediately. It was as though she was waiting for the phone to ring.

'Hello?'

'It's Sarah. Where are you? We thought we were meeting you in the hotel lobby.'

'We've been sitting here for the last hour,' came the reply. 'I've been phoning Polly and left a message.'

'She's left her phone in her room,' Sarah informed her.

'I don't understand. We're in the hotel lobby,' insisted Maggie.

'You can't be. We're sitting in the hotel lobby.'

'What's up?' asked Polly, curious as to how the conversation was going.

'Maggie says they're in the hotel lobby.'

Polly looked round. The hotel was tiny and it would be

impossible not to be able to see them. Sarah put the call on speaker so that Polly could join in.

'Where are you sitting?' asked Polly.

'By the concierge desk,' replied Maggie.

'What's she talking about, concierge desk?' Sarah looked blankly at Polly. Other than a couple of sofas there was nothing else.

'There's no concierge desk,' repeated Sarah, totally mystified as to where Maggie and Lizzy could be.

'What hotel are you in?' came an obvious question from Maggie.

'The Brown Hotel,' replied Sarah.

There was a pause, some discussion with someone in the background, and then Sarah and Polly could hear laughter at the other end of the phone.

'Looks like we might have booked the wrong hotel,' Maggie said in between laughter. 'We booked The Brown. Apparently we're on the other side of town to where you are. Oops.'

Polly laughed as she recalled the mix-up. She reached into her handbag. The pastry that she had secreted earlier at breakfast was starting to call her name so she decided to eat it.

'I can't believe you're still hungry,' commented Sarah.

'I'm not really. It's just that I know it's there so I've got to eat it.'

'Me too,' said a voice behind them. Lizzy had overheard Polly and Sarah talking as she started to tuck into her contraband. 'And don't forget about the problems Maggie had with her hotel room,' said Lizzy, in between mouthfuls.

Polly smiled. The whole trip had been a bit of a disaster

and Maggie and Lizzy clearly wished they had booked into the correct hotel. Not only did Maggie have to change rooms because none of the electrics seemed to work, she also noticed a strange smell in her new room. This became even more obvious when she got into bed and as she rolled over, much to her shock, she noticed the smell was coming from the mattress. She leapt out of bed and rushed downstairs to see the concierge, who seemed rather bemused at the sight of her in her pyjamas.

'It smells like someone has died in my room,' she spluttered.

He looked somewhat alarmed. 'I'm sorry, madam. Did you say someone has died in your room?'

'No. It smells as though someone has. There's a really strange smell and it's coming from my mattress.'

The concierge looked relieved. He didn't relish the thought of having to phone for an ambulance and the police in the middle of the night, least of all on his shift. 'I'm sure they haven't. Let me see if we have another room for you to stay in.' He looked at the records on the computer and found another room for her. 'We've only got a junior suite available, I'm afraid. Would you like to stay there tonight?'

'As long as everything works in the room and there's no strange smell,' replied Maggie. She was too exhausted to have a discussion about it after a busy day sightseeing. She just wanted to get to bed and have some sleep.

'I will send someone up to move all your belongings.'

'Don't bother,' interrupted Maggie. 'I'll sort all that out in the morning. I'm too tired to repack everything now.' She took the key and headed to her new room, which was quite an improvement on the last two rooms she had stayed in.

Lizzy felt quite jealous of Maggie the following morning when she went to have a look round her suite and help her move all her belongings. 'Very nice,' she commented as she tried out the sofa in the room.

'Do you think someone died in that other room?'

'They're not saying. For some reason the room has been closed off for the past few months. No idea why.'

'Perhaps it was to try and get rid of the smell.'

'Well, that certainly failed. All I know is I'm glad I'm not sleeping in that bed. It still gives me the creeps thinking about it.'

Lizzy recounted the whole story. Every time she told it the story became more and more elaborate, but it was extremely entertaining.

April interrupted their reminiscing as the coach pulled into the carpark. 'Enjoy the craft fair, ladies. Don't spend too much money.' She smiled. Bob gave her a sideways glance which she chose to ignore. 'We're leaving here at two o'clock, so please be prompt, and don't eat too much lunch as we've got a cream tea booked for later this afternoon.'

There were sounds of approval from the ladies, who made a quick exit from the coach and headed to the fair.

There was so much to buy that Polly felt she was like a child in a sweet-shop. She couldn't make up her mind what she wanted so she didn't buy anything. Sarah, on the other hand, decided to buy some very early Christmas presents.

'You're so organised.' Polly was impressed.

'It's the only way I can cope with Christmas.'

On the one occasion that Polly had been organised enough to buy an early present she then 'lost' it. She was so impressed that she had bought a present a few months early for Mark. She hid it so well as she didn't want him to find it, that she couldn't find it either. It was only six months after Christmas when she was going through some of her 'stuff' for a competition that she discovered Mark's Christmas present. That was the last time she was that organised.

'Aren't you buying anything, Polly?' Sarah couldn't believe that Polly could attend an event like this and leave with nothing.

'No. Thought I'd give my bank account a rest, although there's loads of amazing stuff here.'

'What about you, Lizzy?'

'Seen a lovely scarf that I might treat myself to. Did you find out any more about Gillian and her missing husband?' Lizzy asked out of the blue.

'Why do you ask?' Polly was curious as to what had prompted this question.

'Just saw her over there with Margery.'

'Oh yes.' Polly spotted her. 'Wonder if Margery has sold any more pot plants.'

Lizzy looked puzzled.

'What? Don't you know?'

'Know what?'

'Some of the plants she sold at club were cannabis. The secret ingredient in Edna's cake was pot!'

'No!'

Sarah glared at Polly, knowing full well that now that Lizzy knew what had happened it was likely that everyone would.

'Don't tell anyone. I promised Edna I wouldn't let on about any of this.'

'Don't worry, I won't say anything,' replied Lizzy, but Polly could already see Lizzy's brain ticking over about this latest scandal. For a split second she wished she hadn't opened her mouth but it was too late.

'I don't suppose either of you fancy grabbing a bite to eat?' Sarah changed the subject and well aware that the answer was likely to be a resounding 'Yes.'

'Just our luck that we come all the way to this craft fair and bump into members from my flower club.' Margery was unimpressed when she caught a glimpse of some familiar faces. She was desperately hoping she wouldn't bump into Edna. She still hadn't got over the audacity of her making an unexpected visit to check out her plants.

'I suppose it's only to be expected. Bet they've been to the flower festival,' replied Gillian, just pleased to be away from Charles for a couple of days.

'You're probably right. This is a very small world after all.'

'Not wanting to spoil our day further, but I thought I should let you know that I've suggested to Charles that he pays you a visit.'

'Why on earth did you do that?' Margery was shocked.

'Can you treat him with herbs the way you did Robert and Henry?' Gillian ignored Margery's question.

'If I must.'

'Don't be like that.'

'I'm sorry, Gillian. I just can't stand the man.'

'Well, we're agreed on that matter.'

'I can remember a time when you were totally besotted.'

'That's a very distant memory for me. I know it sounds wicked, but I wish it was him who'd died and not Robert. The more I dislike Charles, the more I realise how much I loved Robert.'

Margery agreed. 'It's funny that by comparison Robert wasn't too bad a husband.'

'Absolutely not.'

'Why do you want me to treat him?' Margery was curious.

'He's getting lots of headaches recently and seems more irritable than usual. I was hoping you had something that might calm him down a bit and make him a bit less argumentative.'

'And he's happy to see me?'

'Yes. There's no way he'll see a doctor. You know what men are like.'

Margery nodded. 'Only too well.'

'I told him that you might be able to give him some herbs that will help with the headaches and surprisingly he seemed quite amenable.' Gillian wasn't too surprised. She had the distinct impression that Charles rather liked Margery but she wasn't going to tell her that.

'Send him along and I'll see what I can do.' Margery looked round the marquee. 'No sign of Edna.'

Gillian laughed. 'She's not that bad.'

'She is when she's telling you off. In fact she's quite scary.'

'Well, you were a bit naughty turning up at flower club with *those* plants.'

Margery smiled. Had she given the matter a bit more thought she could probably have predicted Edna's response. It certainly hadn't been her intention to shock anyone.

'You're lucky you haven't got into trouble growing them.' Gillian was concerned. 'I think you could end up in prison if anyone reported you.' She was well aware that Margery hadn't taken this seriously at all. She seemed to treat the whole matter as a bit of a joke.

'That's not going to happen.' Margery dismissed Gillian's concerns, although Gillian wasn't so sure.

They'd had an enjoyable, albeit slightly pricey, lunch.

'They've got a captive audience, haven't they?' noted Polly.

'And it's all organic, so that automatically means it'll cost more,' chipped in Sarah.

'Still, at least it filled a hole,' commented Lizzy, despite having eaten her two pastries before she had arrived at the craft fair.

'Best get back on the coach.' Polly helped Sarah carry numerous bags full of early Christmas shopping.

Polly laughed. 'Doubt Bob will be too impressed when he sees this lot,' she said as she looked at all Sarah's purchases.

'Tough,' replied Sarah. 'Mind you, I think I'll feel happier taking this lot on the coach. I don't want anything getting crushed. What do you think?'

'I'm sure we can fit it in somehow,' replied Polly as she carefully started filling the luggage rack with the bags.

As soon as everything was loaded up the coach set off.

'Bang on time.' Bob was pleased that everyone was complying with the timetable and that no one had been left behind.

It was a short drive to the garden centre and yet more eating and spending money. Despite only eating lunch a short time ago Polly was ready for her cream tea. She sat down at a table with Sarah and Lizzy. Jennifer hovered nearby. 'Would you mind if I join you?' she asked.

Polly was a little disappointed as she wanted to gossip with Sarah and Lizzy but felt obliged to let her sit with them as everyone else seemed to have settled down and there were no obvious spare seats. 'Of course you can,' she replied, trying to smile.

'Sorry about your exhibit getting disqualified at the last show,' said Lizzy, without thinking that this could sound extremely insensitive.

Jennifer looked a little embarrassed.

'Well, I for one thought your design was lovely,' said Sarah, trying to take the pressure off Jennifer.

'Thank you, Sarah. That's kind of you to say.'

'Me too,' chipped in Polly. 'It's a shame the judges weren't happy.'

Before Lizzy could put in her two-penn'orth, Sarah changed the subject.

'Did you buy anything at the craft fair this morning, Jennifer?'

'Nothing really. What about you?'

'Sarah bought her Christmas presents,' interrupted Polly before Sarah could respond.

'I'm very impressed,' replied Jennifer as the waitress appeared and set up a plate of fruit scones with clotted cream and strawberry jam in front of her.

'Wonder if these are home-made,' commented Polly as she scrutinised the produce before her. She took a bite from one half of a scone that was heavily laden with cream and jam.

'Well?' asked Lizzy, curious as to Polly's verdict.

'I think it is home-made, although if Edna was here I'm sure she would have something to say about it not being moist enough.'

Sarah smiled. 'I'm not that fussed, they look delicious if

you ask me.' She took her scone before Polly or Lizzy could get in for second helpings.

No sooner was the cream tea served than it had been consumed by everyone.

'Shame we only get one scone each,' commented Lizzy as she picked up every crumb from her plate with a finger.

'Come on, you two. Let's go round the garden centre and see what bargains we can find,' suggested Sarah before Polly and Lizzy could order more cakes.

It came as no surprise to Bob when he saw the ladies returning to the coach a short time later, laden down with plants and yet more carrier bags.

Polly had found a plant that she just had to have although she had no idea where she would put it in her garden. 'I've been looking for one of these for ages,' she said, trying to justify the purchase.

'You do realise that it grows very big,' pointed out Sarah.

'I'll just have to keep an eye on it and if it gets too big I'll prune it. Though I'm planning on cutting lots off it for my flower arrangements, so it might be OK.' Polly wasn't going to accept that there might be a problem.

The coach was extremely quiet for a large part of the journey home as the ladies thought about their trip away.

April pulled out the microphone once again. 'Good afternoon, ladies. This is your afternoon wake-up call,' she joked as she glanced round the coach to see that a lot of the ladies appeared to have nodded off to sleep. There was some laughter as the ladies realised that they might have dropped off for a short time.

'Shall we do the raffle now?' April had worked extremely hard to ensure that this trip was a success and had donated a lot of the raffle prizes herself. All were wrapped up so that no one knew what they were. It was very much a lucky dip.

The first number out of the hat belonged to Jennifer. April selected one of the packages and passed it to Lizzy to pass backwards down the coach to where Jennifer was sitting. The next number was called and another package was sent towards the back of the coach. It wasn't long before several packages were wending their way along both sides of the coach in search of the lucky winners.

By the time all the raffle prizes were distributed, the coach was pulling into its final destination and bang on time. Mark was waiting to meet Polly and Sarah at the agreed pick-up point. He laughed when he saw them both struggling with the cases and bags.

'Can you help with this lot?' called out Polly, aware that there was still more 'stuff' to unload.

'You've only been away for one night. How on earth could you buy so many things?' Mark wasn't too surprised, he'd seen it all before but it never ceased to amaze him how much Polly could buy. She handed him the shrub she'd bought. 'Where's that going?' he asked.

'If we put it on its side it can go in the boot,' replied Polly.

'No, when we get home. There's no room in the garden.'

'Don't worry about that. I'll find room somehow. I just had to have this as I've wanted one of these for ages.'

Mark wasn't going to argue with her. The garden was very much Polly's domain. As far as he was concerned if she thought she could fit it in, she probably could. He looked enquiringly at the dung beetle.

'I bought that for you.'

'Dare I ask what it is?' To Mark it was unrecognisable.

'A dung beetle of course.'

'Of course. How silly of me not to have known that,' Mark replied sarcastically. 'Just what I've always wanted. I've always wondered what was missing from my life all these years. I'll be the envy of the neighbourhood.'

'Exactly. Now your life is complete,' said Polly, laughing. Mark smiled. He wasn't surprised at Polly's purchase as she did have a habit of buying some rather strange objects. He put it in the car.

'Sarah's done all her Christmas shopping,' commented Polly as she handed Mark the numerous carrier bags.

'Really?' He was impressed.

'Not all of it, just a few bits and pieces,' Sarah informed him, pleased with herself for being able to cross a few items off her list already.

'Had a good time?' Mark asked them as he drove Sarah home.

'It was great. No real disasters,' said Polly.

Mark laughed. 'That's always good news, though with you two I never know what's going to happen.'

EIGHTEEN

Rose had worked well into the night getting ready for the supermarket charity event the following day. The manager of the store had kindly donated a dozen bunches of flowers so that Rose could put together some flower arrangements to sell for the charity.

As Rose worked her way through the bunches of flowers, she realised that perhaps she had made a mistake arranging to hold the charity sale the day after the flower festival in Winchester. Had she booked it for another weekend not only could she have gone to Winchester, she could probably have enlisted some help to make the arrangements. But there was no way she was going to admit to Edna that she had got it wrong.

She glanced at her watch. It was fast approaching midnight and she felt exhausted. By then her dining-room table was completely covered with small arrangements, and several were on the floor surrounding it. Relieved she had done as much as she possibly could do that day she headed for bed. She fell asleep almost before her head hit the pillow.

It felt as though she had only just got into bed when her alarm sounded and it was time to get up and start loading her car.

Polly groaned as her alarm went off. She wished that she hadn't volunteered to help Rose but, judging by the reaction at the committee meeting, she didn't want to let her down. Mark was still fast asleep as she got out of bed and quietly got dressed before heading downstairs for some breakfast.

She laughed to herself as she looked out of the living-room window on to her lawn and noticed that Mark had put the dung beetle right in the centre of it.

As soon as she had finished breakfast, she headed over to the supermarket where Rose was already setting up their table. It looked spectacular.

'You've been busy,' commented Polly as she watched Rose arranging the various designs on the table. There were a selection of flower arrangements; some were in baskets, others in plastic dishes, but all looked quite stunning.

'Yes, I have. How was the flower show?'

'Lovely. Got some great ideas,' replied Polly as she started putting out the leaflets advertising the flower club. She pulled out the club notice board that had photos of a number of their exhibits.

'Looking good,' said Sarah as she headed into the supermarket lobby. 'You've done a fantastic job, Rose, well done.'

'Thought it made sense to get these made in advance rather than making them this morning, as we've no idea how busy we're going to be.' She glanced over towards the door and saw April and Hilary staggering in with an armful of garden foliage.

'That's great. We needed some more foliage. Put it in the bucket.' Rose pointed to the bucket she had placed behind the table. 'Thanks for coming along.'

'Well, we couldn't just leave you to it. Where do you want us?' asked Hilary.

'It would be good if someone hands out our leaflets and tries to recruit some new members. Sarah, would you mind selling the arrangements?'

'Fine by me.'

'Where do you want me?' asked Polly, feeling slightly concerned that Rose might want her to do some hand-tied designs.

'Why don't you help Sarah sell the arrangements but help me out if I get snowed under?' suggested Rose.

'Sounds good to me.' She felt slightly relieved and hoped that Rose was able to cope with any demand for bouquet orders.

It wasn't long before the first shoppers started to appear. They seemed quite taken by the beautiful display of flowers that greeted them as they entered the store.

'Can I interest you ladies in buying one of our arrangements?' asked Sarah, keen to make her first sale.

'Are you flower arrangers?' asked Hilary.

'No.'

'Would you be interested in coming along to our flower club? We meet once a month in the church hall.'

'It's great fun,' chipped in Polly before they had a chance to answer. 'You don't have to be a flower arranger to come along.'

'If you're free for our next meeting why don't you come along and give us a try?' suggested Hilary.

They weren't sure whether or not either of these ladies would come along, but at least they had extended the invitation.

'Just a suggestion,' observed Rose. 'Perhaps it would be better if you don't all tackle the same customer. It might be a bit intimidating if they're surrounded.' Rose had a point. They were hoping to recruit new members, not put them off attending.

Five or ten minutes passed with no one coming near, then a lady looked over in their direction, clearly interested as to what they had on sale. She walked over to them and examined all the arrangements. 'These are such lovely arrangements,' she commented as she made up her mind which one she wanted to purchase. As soon as she had bought one, the table was suddenly surrounded by Sunday shoppers all keen for a bargain.

'You're welcome to buy one of our arrangements, or if you would like to purchase some flowers in the supermarket we would be pleased to wrap them for you,' announced Rose. Several people decided to take Rose up on her offer and shortly appeared with bunches of flowers to be wrapped. Rose worked as fast as she could but Polly realised she was going to have to help.

The first bouquet she made wasn't too bad. She incorporated several pieces of foliage into it, and by her standards she thought it looked acceptable, even if it did take a while for her to make it. Sarah intervened and chatted to the person in order to distract them from the fact that Polly was incredibly slow and the air was somewhat blue as Polly swore under her breath. The customer seemed very pleased with the finished result and Polly gained some confidence from this. However, the next request wasn't straightforward. She was asked to make a bouquet out of a dozen roses and no foliage. For anyone who has made a bouquet they will know that rose stems slip and having a piece or two of foliage helps prevent this.

Polly spiralled the stems, once, then twice, then thrice. She keep undoing them, and starting again. No matter how many times she attempted making this bouquet it just wouldn't work.

'Help,' whispered Polly to Rose, hoping that the customer didn't hear her. She could see that the customer was becoming frustrated with her. Rose took hold of the roses and in a few movements had them looking perfect. She handed them to Polly to wrap and give them to a relieved customer, who was starting to get into a panic over the amount of time she had left on her car-parking permit.

Edna had started to feel guilty about not volunteering to help and, as she needed to do some shopping, she decided she would visit the supermarket.

'George, will you come shopping with me?' George was surprised at the invitation. Usually Edna wanted to go shopping on her own as she didn't trust George to do her shopping for her.

'Why?' He was curious.

'I want to go and check out the flower sale that some of my committee are doing, but I don't want to get stuck with helping. If you're with me, they won't expect me to help.'

'So, you're using me?'

'In a way.' Edna laughed. 'I just want to know what's happening.'

'Being nosey you mean?'

'Yes, exactly.'

Edna got her coat and picked up her car keys and George

and Edna set off for the supermarket. By the time they arrived, Rose was snowed under. The flower arrangements were being bought faster than she could make them.

Edna was pleasantly surprised by what she saw. Hilary spotted her. 'Glad you could come.'

'We're just passing so we thought we'd drop in and see how you're getting on.'

'Great. We've been incredibly busy. Sold loads.'

'Any interest in the flower club?'

'Not sure. We've handed out a lot of leaflets but you never know.'

Polly noticed Edna talking to Hilary. 'Look who's turned up.' She muttered to Rose.

'Come to check us out, no doubt.'

'Funny she didn't offer to help. I thought she was away or something, but obviously not.'

'I don't think she wanted to come because it wasn't her idea.' Rose felt quite bitter.

'For heaven's sake.' Polly couldn't believe Edna could behave like that.

'It's true. She was miffed with me arranging this.'

'I can't handle that kind of behaviour.' Polly had little respect for anyone who behaved like that. 'At the end of the day we're raising money for charity. That's more than she's done all year. If we waited for her to arrange anything, we'd never raise any money.'

'Exactly.' Rose turned to a customer. 'Can I help you?'

'Can you wrap these flowers, please?' she asked.

Polly walked over to where Edna was. 'Rose has done incredibly well, don't you think?' she asked.

Edna was loath to admit it, but Polly was correct. What

Edna thought was going to be a damp squib had turned into a success story, judging by how busy they were.

'Best get going. Need to get a few bits of shopping, then we're going out for lunch,' Edna responded, although George looked somewhat surprised by the mention of lunch.

'Where are we going, dear?' he asked, concerned that his memory had failed him.

'Nowhere. I wanted them to think that we had something planned, otherwise they would wonder why I didn't stay,' replied Edna, 'although you can always take me out for lunch if you want to.'

It had been a long time since they had treated themselves to a meal out and George was interested in trying out a new French restaurant that had opened a couple of miles down the road. 'Let's try that new place then.'

Edna was pleased with the result. Not only had the flower club raised some awareness this morning, plus money for the charity, without her having to lift a finger, but also she was being treated to lunch. She headed off with George.

There was a constant stream of people all morning but by lunch-time the flow had definitely waned, and with no more arrangements left to sell, Rose decided to call it a day. 'Think we should pack up now,' she suggested, much to Polly's relief. She was clearly flagging after her busy weekend.

There was little to clear up other than a few dishes and floral foam which were quickly gathered up and put in Rose's car. The foliage left over was repossessed by Hilary to use at a function later that week, for which she had volunteered to do some floral designs.

It wasn't long before Polly was back home and fast asleep on the sofa.

NINETEEN

Seeing Charles standing on her doorstop wasn't something Margery had been looking forward to, but Gillian was insistent that Margery should help find a remedy for him.

Charles seemed to be totally unaware of Margery's feelings towards him and had been quite looking forward to seeing her. She intrigued him with all her potions and in his eyes she was extremely knowledgeable. She showed him into her dining-room and he sat down at the table.

'Now what seems to be the problem?' she asked him in quite a professional way, trying not to let any personal feelings enter her mind.

'I'm having a lot of headaches these days.'

'Any particular time of day?'

'No. They come on whenever they like. Sometimes in the middle of the night.'

Charles went into great detail about these headaches and how he felt generally so that Margery got a good idea of what was happening. He didn't seem to want to leave despite

Margery's hints that she didn't need any more information. For a second she felt quite uncomfortable with him, as though he was flirting with her. He seemed totally oblivious to the fact that Margery couldn't stand him and that she was only being polite to please Gillian. He finally took the hint and picked up his keys and headed for home. Margery gave a sigh of relief.

Margery needed to have a good think about what to give Charles before she mixed up a concoction for him. She said she'd get it to him within a few days, although she was hoping that she might be able to meet up with Gillian rather than having to have Charles round again.

She looked at her various jars of dried herbs and seeds. When she had treated Robert and Henry she had found it relatively easy to choose a remedy for them. However, Charles was a completely different story.

Henry had come to her with indigestion. Diagnosis wasn't too difficult for her. Henry rushed about all the time and lived on his nerves. His stomach often felt twisted and gripy but Margery was sure this was down to stress. She made up a concoction of peppermint and camomile to try and settle things down. Robert had only ever consulted her for his travel sickness which was easy to prescribe for.

Margery had really developed a love for herbs since Duncan had died. She would often go out walking in the countryside and picked plants to be dried for future use. However, her inability to remember the names of plants and fully recognise them was putting her and her patients in a dangerous position.

It was only when a friend popped round and noticed a bunch of hemlock drying that Margery started to doubt her ability.

'Isn't that hemlock?' asked her friend, quite innocently.

'I think so,' Margery replied, not aware that there was a problem with having this.

'But that's deadly poisonous, isn't it?'

Margery felt embarrassed. She didn't want to admit that she didn't know what she was doing. 'Only in large doses. Besides, you don't eat it,' she lied, trying to cover up for the fact that she didn't understand herbs that fully.

Her explanation seemed to satisfy her friend but as soon as she had gone Margery got the herbal book down from the shelf to research it. 'Water hemlock is an extremely poisonous plant,' she read.

Oh dear, she thought. *That was a lucky escape.* She threw the hemlock away. This incident knocked her confidence quite a lot but not enough for her to stop prescribing herbs she didn't really understand.

It wasn't long after that Henry collapsed and died of a heart attack. It came as a complete shock for both Gillian and Margery, who thought he was just suffering from indigestion. Gillian wondered if perhaps Henry should have seen a doctor, rather than Margery, as she was aware that Margery sometimes got her herbs mixed up. But Margery had been her friend for years and she didn't challenge her on this.

Margery selected a number of her herbs and weighed them out. She wasn't exactly sure what to give Charles, but thought that a mixture of feverfew, chamomile, and some of her secret ingredients, might help him. Once she was satisfied she had the right mixture she bagged the herbs up, added a herbal tincture and phoned Gillian to give her the news. Much to her relief, Gillian agreed to meet her for a cup of coffee, so at least Margery wouldn't have to be alone with Charles again.

TWENTY

orna had been looking forward to her garden party for some time. In her eyes, there was nothing better than showing off to people. The garden was pristine; all the shrubs were neatly cut back and, despite his protests, Stuart was made to mow the lawn one last time. He never questioned Lorna's instructions, but on this occasion he thought it was overkill to mow the lawn again. It already looked as neat as the Wimbledon lawns at the start of the tennis championship.

It had been decided that the gazebos would be erected on the south side of the lawn, which was the least attractive area, as Lorna didn't want to spoil the main part of the lawn. That area got so much sun that the lawn always looked a bit dried and bleached by midsummer.

Stuart had managed to locate the gazebos in the loft, although some had definitely seen better days. He unpacked them and set about trying to assemble them, which was close to impossible on his own.

'Lorna, can you help me?' he called out. She didn't

particularly want to get her hands dirty but knew that this was the only way she would get the job done.

Lorna had enlisted most of the flower club committee to help set up and run the event for her, with the exception of Lizzy and Julia who had made their excuses. She was relieved to see Hilary and Rose arrive. 'Can you come over here?' she called out to them. They did as they were told and within minutes of arriving they had been given the task of assisting Stuart with putting up the gazebos.

Barbara arrived and noticed a table and chair already in the front garden beside the side gate. 'I've put that there for you, Barbara,' Lorna informed her. 'I thought you could collect the tickets and any outstanding money. Plus stop any gate-crashers. Can someone sell raffle tickets?'

'No problem.' Barbara was content to sit out the front and keep away from the chaos that was likely to ensue in the kitchen. She was quite amused by Lorna's suggestion that she should stop gate-crashers. With only thirty tickets sold, and most of those to other clubs, a few gate-crashers would be welcome. They hadn't told Lorna about the poor ticket sales to their club members and secretly hoped that a few more would turn up.

As soon as Freda arrived, Barbara collared her. 'Would you be able to sell raffle tickets, Freda?' she asked before Freda could even take her jacket off.

Freda had a quick look at the raffle prizes. They were hardly appealing. Most had done the rounds at other raffles. Freda was sure that she had seen some of them at least a few times before.

When Polly and Sarah arrived they were slightly stressed. 'Had terrible trouble parking. Didn't realise there were parking restrictions on a weekend.'

'Ridiculous, isn't it?' commented Barbara. 'Have you got your tickets?'

'Yes, but it's a bit stupid that the committee has to pay to come in considering we're the ones doing all the work.'

'That was Edna's idea. Not sure I totally agree with her.'

'Is she here yet?' Sarah looked round. It was always interesting seeing Edna and Lorna together. To say that they rubbed each other up the wrong way was an understatement. Both tried to out-smart each other with their bragging.

'I'm knackered. What with being away last weekend, then the charity stall on Sunday,' commented Polly.

'It's full-on at the moment. Shame these events weren't spaced out a bit more,' agreed Sarah.

'Can I interest you in a raffle ticket?' Freda asked, interrupting them, although she already knew the answer.

'No thanks.' Polly Laughed. 'Can't believe that old handbag has turned up again as a raffle prize. I think it was donated by Margery about five years ago.'

'Dreadful, isn't it? But we were struggling to find enough prizes this time round.'

'Good luck.' Sarah smiled at Freda as she and Polly made their way to the back garden.

Lorna was ready to pounce and give out her orders. 'Good to see you two. I'm putting you on kitchen duty,' she informed them.

'Great,' Polly replied sarcastically.

'Can you get all these cakes out on plates and sort out the teapots and teacups?' instructed Lorna before she headed further down the garden to check on the progress of the gazebos.

Sarah gazed out of the kitchen window and started laughing.

'What's up?' enquired Polly, curious as to what Sarah saw that was so funny.

'Look at them trying to get that gazebo up.'

Although it was quite a sunny day there was a definite breeze which seemed to be getting stronger and, despite Hilary and Rose helping Stuart, they struggled to assemble the last gazebo. Every time they got it into position a gust of wind intervened.

Lorna was beginning to stress. 'Just hold it tight, Stuart,' she ordered, but even she couldn't control nature. Eventually they accepted that they weren't meant to put this one up and had to make do with the ones already in place.

Hilary and Rose then started setting up the table and chairs. Rose looked in the direction of the kitchen and spotted Sarah and Polly laughing. She pulled a face before getting back on with her job. Edna appeared at the kitchen door loaded down with cake tins and boxes. 'Looks like you've been busy,' commented Polly as she helped her carry the tins and placed them on the work surface.

'Wasn't sure how many to bake. After all, there aren't that many people coming but at least everyone will have a choice.'

'What have you baked?' Polly was desperate to see inside the tins.

'Apple cake, lemon drizzle, chocolate brownies and a coconut cake. And no, before you ask, I haven't made one of my happy cakes!'

'All sounds great. I wouldn't mind trying all of those.' Polly knew that as she had been landed with kitchen duty she would probably try all the cakes. Just a perk of the job. She started putting slices of the cakes out on to the highly-decorated bone china plates that Lorna had provided for her to use.

Edna decided that perhaps she should head into the garden to see Lorna, who was still giving out orders to her husband. Lorna spotted her. 'Edna. How lovely to see you,' she called out, although it was quite insincere.

'Hello, Lorna. How's it going?'

'Fine. Just putting the finishing touches to everything,' she replied, although she wasn't putting any finishing touches to anything as she had enlisted everyone else's help to do this. She headed into the house. 'I'm just getting changed and I'll be back down in a few minutes.'

By the time she returned a number of people had arrived for the tea party. She wafted past Polly, who had to do a double-take. 'What on earth is she wearing?' she asked Sarah as Lorna flounced into the garden to greet her guests.

Lorna had changed into a rather bright-coloured, long floating kaftan over a pair of wide-legged white trousers. She had no intention of doing any work that afternoon and relished in the thought of showing her garden off to her visitors and being the perfect hostess.

'When do you think we should serve the tea?' Sarah asked, starting to get impatient. More visitors had arrived and had all taken their seats under the limited gazebos, having negotiated their way across the uneven lawn. Polly headed into the garden in an attempt to collar Lorna.

'Lorna? Can we serve tea now?' she asked. Lorna turned round to face her clearly looking slightly put out that someone had interrupted her flow of conversation. She flicked her hand in the air to dismiss Polly. 'Not yet, I'll tell you when,' she said in her best Edinburgh accent.

Polly stormed back into the kitchen. 'I've just had her flick her hand in my face.'

'How rude. Who does she think she is?'

'Lady Muck, by the looks of things.'

'Can we serve tea now?' Sarah dared to ask.

'No. She's going to tell us when.'

'How on earth did we get landed with doing this? What a waste of an afternoon.'

'Fancy a cup of tea?' suggested Polly.

'Is that being naughty?'

'No. We're not going to get any tea once we start serving, so we might as well have a cuppa now and a slice or two of cake to keep our sugar levels up.'

Just as Polly was putting a piece of apple cake on to her plate, Edna walked into the kitchen. Polly looked up at her, feeling rather guilty.

'That woman will be the death of me,' complained Edna, clearly annoyed with Lorna.

'Join the club. Come and have some tea and cake while we're waiting for our orders,' suggested Sarah.

Edna smiled. She hated being rude about people but this time Lorna had pushed her about as far as she could stand. 'Sounds like a good idea to me,' she replied as she helped herself to a slice of her lemon drizzle cake.

Polly was already on to her second slice of cake when the order finally came through from Lorna that tea could be served.

'Freda, do you think you could lend a hand carrying all this stuff?' Polly indicated to the table full of trays of china cups, teapots and plates of cakes. Freda had given up trying to sell raffle tickets and was now at a loose end.

'I'm not sure about that,' she replied. Freda had a habit of tripping over her own feet and the thought of carrying

Lorna's best china down the garden filled her with dread. 'Can't someone else help?' she asked. She usually wore extremely flat shoes but today she had decided to wear her 'high heels'. To most people these were flat shoes but to her, with a two-inch heel, they were extremely high and she felt as though she was tottering around in them. Had she known that she was going to get roped into serving tea and trudging backwards and forwards across the lawn, perhaps she would have been better in her 'old faithfuls' but they didn't look too good with her new floral dress.

'Don't worry about it then. You get the tea made and we'll carry it,' suggested Sarah. The last thing she wanted was for Freda to end up head first in Lorna's prize azalea.

Freda loaded the overfull teapots on to the trays and Polly and Sarah headed off from the kitchen, down the steps, across the patio, over the first lawn and on to the second lawn, which was considerably bumpy by comparison.

'Watch your step, Polly,' Sarah warned her as her own foot got caught in one of the many uneven parts on the lawn.

Polly carefully put the tray down on one of the tables, relieved that she had managed to put it there without too much spillage. She passed all the cups and saucers round the table and one of the guests started to pour the tea.

'Cakes look lovely,' the guest commented. Polly nodded. They did look lovely and to her it was torture having to carry them out for other people to eat when she would love to be waited on hand and foot. She returned to the kitchen and picked up the next tray. Freda had by now got it down to a fine art and was busy organising the distribution of tea and cakes. It took several trips backwards and forwards to the kitchen before everyone had a cup of tea and plate of cakes.

'Polly?' Lorna called out just as Polly was making her way back to the kitchen for a well-deserved rest.

'Yes, Lorna?'

'Would you mind going round to all the tables again and ensure that the teapots are topped up and refill the cake plates?'

Polly couldn't answer her as she was afraid of what words were likely to come out of her mouth. She turned her back on her and walked into the kitchen, seething.

'What's up?' asked Freda, who by now was sitting on one of the high stools enjoying a slice of Edna's coconut cake.

'Lady Muck wants us to go round and refill all the teapots and cake plates.'

'You're joking! Well, I'm going to finish this slice of cake first,' replied Freda, in defiance.

Polly refilled the kettles and sat down at the table to enjoy a third slice of cake and a cup of tea. It wasn't long before Lorna was standing in the doorway. 'Ladies. Can you please look after our guests instead of sitting here eating all the cakes?' she asked. Everyone glared at her.

'All right, Lorna, keep your hair on. We're waiting for the kettle to boil,' replied Polly, before she realised what she had said, and the tone in which she had said it.

Lorna stormed off. She was used to getting her own way and didn't like anyone answering her back.

'Best get out there and refill the teapots,' said Sarah reluctantly. 'We don't want her having a hissy-fit.'

'Too late for that I think.' Polly smiled. 'Well. She really gets on my nerves.'

Freda could see that Lorna had upset Polly. 'Polly, you stay here and get the kettle boiled and I'll help Sarah sort out refilling the teapots and plates.'

'Thanks, Freda,' replied Polly, pleased that she didn't have to face Lorna again for a while. She watched Sarah and Freda head down to the garden. Freda loaded a number of teapots and empty plates on her tray and headed back to the kitchen. As she walked over the uneven ground she tripped slightly but managed to regain her balance. 'That lawn is dreadful,' she said as she entered the kitchen.

'I know. I almost fell over when I was walking over it,' agreed Polly.

Polly loaded up the tray with refreshed teapots, jugs of milk and some more plates of cake and Freda headed straight off, although feeling somewhat nervous about venturing across the uneven lawn once again. Polly reboiled the kettle ready for the next lot of refills.

Suddenly she heard a scream from the garden. She raced to the back door and looked down the garden to see Lorna stomping up and down. Her lovely white trousers now had a distinct brown pattern splashed over them. Sprawled out on the lawn was Freda; the tray of cakes scattered all around her. Lorna's milk jug had managed to find its way under one of the tables and her teapot was precariously perched on the branch of one of her roses.

'I'm so sorry,' said Freda as she got back up and tried to regain her composure. 'I tripped on the lawn.'

'Stupid woman. You should look where you're going,' snapped Lorna.

Edna stood up. She wasn't going to tolerate Lorna being so rude to one of her committee members and long-time friend. 'It's not Freda's fault. This lawn is dreadful. It's hardly surprising that she tripped over.'

'How dare you criticise my lawn,' replied Lorna, furious at Edna's comment.

Sarah intervened. 'Freda, are you all right?' Freda nodded.

'Then let's get back to the tea party. After all, nothing is broken,' Sarah said, trying to reason with Lorna.

'Look at my new trousers. They're ruined.'

'It was an accident, Lorna, nothing more.'

Lorna stormed off into the house, not stopping to speak to Polly who was standing by the doorway, totally speechless with the way the event was unfolding.

The guests were left stunned by her behaviour. They certainly hadn't expected this as entertainment. As soon as Lorna was out of earshot, loud chattering and laughter erupted.

Freda and Sarah returned to the kitchen, having retrieved the teapot, and burst out laughing. 'Did you see what happened?'

Polly nodded. 'Oh yes. I thought there was going to be a punch-up at one stage.'

Edna followed them into the kitchen. 'Are you sure you're all right, Freda?'

'Fine, honestly. Just a bit shaken and shocked.'

'That's hardly surprising with that woman speaking to you like that.'

No sooner had Edna finished her sentence than Lorna reappeared. She had changed into another pair of floating trousers, this time navy blue. She walked straight past all four of them and headed into the garden

'Did you see that?' asked Polly. 'What a cow she is.'

Edna didn't like the way Polly spoke about people but she wasn't going to challenge her. In her eyes, Lorna's behaviour was totally unacceptable and childish.

Seconds after Lorna had left the house, Stuart appeared rather sheepishly at the kitchen door. He had been keeping out of everyone's way by staying in the spare bedroom. He looked somewhat embarrassed and not too sure what to say about Lorna, who by now was flouncing around the garden as if nothing had happened, having witnessed her behaviour from the bedroom window.

'Looks like I missed all the excitement,' he said, smiling, afraid of what reaction he would get.

Edna smiled at him. 'It was quite entertaining, although possibly not for Lorna. We certainly weren't expecting that. Would you like some tea and cake?'

Whilst a lot of the cakes had been eaten, there was still a reasonable selection left. Cake was not something Lorna would allow in the house so this was a real treat for him. He took a couple of slices and headed into the dining-room, out of sight of Lorna.

'Best get back to the party. Have you got the raffle tickets, Freda?' asked Edna.

Freda handed Edna a small carrier bag with all the ticket stubs neatly folded into quarters.

'Lorna, shall we draw the raffle?' Edna called from the doorway. Lorna looked over to her. She didn't appreciate being called to, but in view of everything that had gone on this afternoon, she was in no mood to cause another scene.

'Yes, of course, Edna,' she replied, attempting to put on a smile.

The first few tickets were drawn and the winners chose

their prizes. By then, all the decent prizes had been taken and all that was left were some cheap chocolates, a jar of bath salts, *the* handbag and a make-up bag. Lorna drew the next ticket. There were no takers. 'Come on, ladies, someone must have this ticket.'

No one moved until one of the guests noticed it belonged to a lady sitting next to her. 'Look, it's your ticket.' The woman reluctantly went to collect her prize and looked fairly displeased at the gift she had won.

The next ticket was drawn and again no one came forward. Edna nudged Polly. 'Please say it's your ticket or we could be here all night.'

'I haven't got any tickets.'

'Doesn't matter. You'll be doing everyone a favour. No one wants these remaining prizes.'

Polly put her hand up. 'That's my ticket,' she called out, much to the relief of the other ladies. She picked up the make-up bag which looked as though it had been used on several occasions.

'How many more prizes are there?' Lorna called over to Edna.

'That was the last one,' she lied as she discreetly hid *the* handbag. No doubt it would appear at another raffle in the future.

'Thank you, ladies, for coming this afternoon. I do hope you've enjoyed yourselves and enjoyed seeing my garden.' Lorna launched into her speech. 'Please walk on the paths as you leave,' she ordered. Some of the guests looked surprised at Lorna's instructions.

'Looks like we've outstayed our welcome,' commented one of the ladies.

All the guests started to gather up their belongings and head out of the garden. As instructed, they walked out in single file along the footpath rather than cutting across her pristine lawn. Once everyone had left Lorna went into the house and called out to Stuart.

'Stuart, can you clear the garden?' she ordered. She was surprised to see him leaving the dining-room with an empty plate and a cup and saucer in his hand.

'Yes, dear,' he replied somewhat nervously having been caught out.

Lorna looked at the plate in his hand and the remaining crumbs and guessed that he had helped himself to some tasty morsels, but she was in no mood to argue with him about it. 'Can you get this place tidied up? I'm going to lie down. I feel exhausted.' In a split second she was gone.

Stuart headed into the garden to start dismantling the gazebos. Fortunately they seemed to come down much easier than they went up.

'Where's Lady Muck gone?' Polly asked Freda as she put the make-up bag in the dustbin.

'She's gone to lie down. Obviously it was all a bit too much for her. She said she's exhausted.'

'Poor thing,' replied Polly, sarcastically. 'Suppose we'd better get all this washing-up done.'

'I'll do that, Polly. Any chance you could go and gather up all the cups from the garden? I don't want to go out there again. My feet are killing me.'

Polly looked down at Freda's bare feet and saw that she'd kicked off her shoes. 'That'll teach you not to wear high heels.' Polly laughed as she left the kitchen.

It took a couple of hours to get everything washed up and cleared away.

'Remind me not to volunteer for another one of these. Can't believe I paid a fiver to work my socks off,' moaned Polly.

'Agreed. But it was entertaining,' said Sarah, looking at the bright side.

'That's true. Wouldn't have missed Lorna's tantrum for the world.' Polly dried her hands and picked up her jacket.

Edna smiled as she overheard Polly and Sarah talking. She certainly hadn't expected such an eventful afternoon and couldn't wait to get home to tell George what had happened. 'There's a couple of slices of cake left. Polly, why don't you take them home for all your hard work this afternoon,' she suggested trying to win Polly over.

'Are you sure?' Polly asked as she wrapped up a couple of slices of coconut cake, before Edna changed her mind.

Edna smiled. 'Bye, ladies. See you at club next week,' she said as she gathered up all her cake tins and made her exit.

TWENTY-ONE

Vanda arrived early and was already sitting in the carpark waiting for someone to arrive, which took Edna by surprise as she was usually the first to get to the hall.

'Good evening,' Edna said as politely as she could, although she was clearly annoyed that Vanda had got there so early. 'I'm Edna, club chairman.'

'Hello. I was hoping to get in early as I have a lot to prepare,' Vanda replied, ignoring any niceties.

'Unfortunately, we don't have access to the hall before 7 p.m. I was under the impression that Julia mentioned this to you when she booked you to come and do the demonstration.' Edna knew that Vanda was trying to pull a fast one and it was clear that Vanda wasn't going to listen to instructions from anyone. She opened the boot of her car and started unloading. She handed some of the boxes of flowers to Edna. Edna wasn't used to unloading cars. She usually liked to flit about, checking that everyone was doing their pre-assigned tasks and set up the cake table, rather than actually getting involved with manual work. However, as she was the first of the committee to arrive she didn't have much choice in the matter. She carried a box of flowers into the hall and put it down on the stage.

Vanda didn't look too happy when she saw the size of the stage. It was more like a step rather than a stage, as it was so tiny.

'You can keep your flowers in this side room if you want to.' Edna ignored Vanda's reaction and pointed out a narrow corridor that led off from the stage towards the kitchen. Much to Edna's relief, Julia arrived a few minutes later.

'Sorry, I wasn't expecting you to arrive this early. I thought I had mentioned to you that we couldn't gain access until 7 p.m.,' she commented as tactfully as possible to Vanda.

'I need time to set myself up and get into the zone,' she replied. Julia stifled her laughter. She'd not heard that one before.

Julia saw Polly's car pulling into the carpark space in front of the hall and rushed over to meet her. 'Hello, Polly. Just to let you know that Vanda is already here. She needs time to set herself up and get into the zone.'

'You what?'

'You heard me. She needs to get into the zone. Good luck.' Julia walked off laughing.

Polly proceeded to help Vanda set up the stage with all her 'stuff'. Having been ordered around for a quarter of an hour, she started to realise that there were bossier people in the world than Edna.

She collected Vanda's sandwich from Edna and placed it on a plate, and took this to her along with a cup of coffee. She had ordered a skinny latte but instant coffee with a splash of milk was the limit of the church hall kitchen. Vanda looked at it with some disdain but didn't comment on it. She was too busy getting herself ready to pay much attention to it.

Margery arrived at the hall. She was slightly apprehensive about entering but had decided that Edna wasn't going to put her off selling her plants. She still had a lot to sell so she had decided to go to club and set up her stand. As she entered the hall, Edna spotted her and glanced over in her direction. Margery glared back at her as she proceeded to put her plants out. Edna was desperate to see what she had for sale but decided not to rush over to have a look. She waited patiently while Margery set up and then tried to have a discreet look at the table.

'Nothing to worry about,' said Margery, fully aware that Edna was sussing her out. Edna was relieved that Margery had seen sense and left her pot plants at home.

The members started to arrive and it wasn't long before most of the seats were occupied. When the hall was almost full, Edna went to check on Vanda. 'We're ready to start, Vanda. How many designs are you doing this evening?'

'Six, but I'm not ready to start yet.'

'How much longer do you need?'

'About another half an hour.'

'I'm afraid that's not possible. We have to start now as we have a tea break after three designs and there won't be time to finish if we don't start promptly.'

'Can't you have your tea break now?'

'Not really. I'll go and give out the notices now. That will give you another five minutes or so.' Edna wasn't going to be dictated to and walked away before Vanda could comment. She'd just about had enough of Vanda's attitude and nothing was going to make Edna change the way she did things.

Edna opened the meeting. 'It's nice to see so many of you here tonight. We've got a couple of visitors here this evening, so a really warm welcome to you. I'm sure you're going to have a lovely evening. Just a few notices before we start. Thank you to those of you who attended Lorna's garden party. We had a lovely afternoon.' There was a snigger from a member of the audience who had heard what had happened.

'It would be lovely to see more of you attend an event in the future as our members were greatly outnumbered by non flower club ladies,' she continued, without batting an eyelid.

'A big thank you to April for organising such a wonderful trip to Winchester flower festival. Sadly I couldn't be there, but I heard it was a tremendous success. Well done also to everyone who helped with the charity flower sale at the supermarket. I believe £100 was raised, which was great.' There was a general muttering of approval amongst the audience.

'We should also congratulate Polly and Sarah for doing so well at the recent flower competition. You both did us proud.'

Edna looked over her shoulder to see if Vanda was ready to begin. She was standing to the side of the stage, waiting to make a big entrance. 'Let me introduce our demonstrator this evening, who is Vanda Monroe.'

There was a round of applause as Vanda warily made her way on to the stage and tried not to trip over anything. She squeezed behind the table that had been positioned on the edge of the stage where her first design was going to be set up. She began by giving a great explanation as to what she was going to do that evening, although she had such a strong accent it was difficult to understand what she was saying.

Barbara could feel laughter coming on. 'What did she say?' She turned to Polly who was sitting next to her.

'No idea.' Polly smiled. She whispered to Sarah, 'What's she going on about?'

'Something about flowers,' replied Sarah. Polly passed this useless piece of information to Barbara, who started to chuckle. 'Glad I'm not the only one who hasn't got a clue what's going on.'

'Shh,' Edna snapped over her shoulder.

Barbara pulled a face at Polly, which was the worst thing she could have done. 'Now you've got me in trouble,' she mouthed to her.

The first design was completed and the room erupted into applause.

By now Polly was on the brink of having one of her 'moments' when everything seemed funny. She tried to stifle her laughter but tears started to well up in her eyes and roll down her cheeks. She struggled to keep her laughter in check during the next two designs and, much to her relief, before she made a complete fool of herself, Edna announced the tea break.

'That's good timing,' observed Sarah, knowing full well that Polly's laughter was infectious and when she was having a 'moment' Sarah invariably had one too.

'Fancy a cuppa?' asked Polly.

'Ta.'

'Cake?'

'Surprise me.'

Polly eagerly headed to the cake table to see what goodies were available. Disappointment filled her when she saw a bought cake.

With everything that was going on this evening, Edna hadn't had a chance to inspect the cakes when they were brought in by one of the members. She was shocked by what she saw and knew what Polly was thinking. She pre-empted her saying anything.

'I know. I'm furious about this,' she said, blowing it out of proportion as she had a habit of doing. 'Pamela had her name on the rota to bake and she bought a shop cake,' continued Edna. 'This is ridiculous. Had I known I could have baked something,' she spat out.

'Me too,' Polly agreed with her. Polly gathered up two cups of tea and returned to her seat.

'What, no cake?' asked Sarah, intrigued as to why Polly hadn't selected anything for her.

'Nope. Unless you want shop-bought cake from the supermarket.'

'Not really,' replied Sarah, although she could see the funny side of this situation. 'Can't help it if we've become cake connoisseurs.' She laughed.

'If you're going to eat naughty calories you might as well enjoy them. I'm not wasting any on a shop-bought cake.'

'Here, here,' chipped in Lizzy, who was equally disappointed.

Edna spotted Pamela across the room and headed straight for her. Pamela could see from Edna's expression that she was not happy about something. 'If you've put your name on the cake register, in future can you kindly bake a cake and not buy it?' Edna snapped at Pamela.

Pamela looked surprised at Edna's rudeness. After all, this was hardly a matter that deserved such attention. Had it been anyone else speaking to her in this manner she would have stood her ground and challenged them but Edna had a way of making people feel intimidated. 'I'm sorry,' she heard herself stuttering. 'I had to work late last night and didn't have time to bake. It won't happen again.' Edna seemed satisfied with this explanation.

Pamela made a mental note to herself not to put her name down on the rota again. Edna made a mental note not to let Pamela put her name down again, or if she did she would need to remind her of the responsibility of this action.

As everyone had finished the tea break early Edna called the group to order and Vanda continued her demonstration.

It wasn't long before a lot of commotion was heard going on in the entrance to the church hall. The scouts had their meeting on the same evening as the flower club and they often caused a lot of noise. Edna had already had to put her head round the door this evening to tell them to be quiet, only to be greeted by the sight of a group of scouts play-fighting. But now the noise was considerably louder and an alarm could be heard.

Vanda wasn't used to working in these conditions and was unimpressed by the interruption. 'What on earth is that now?' asked Edna, clearly annoyed that once again their evening had been interrupted. The door opened and the scout master put his head around the door. He looked slightly awkward at having fifty ladies all looking at him. Edna raised her eyebrows.

'I'm afraid you need to leave the hall. That's the fire alarm.' He signalled to the sound coming out of the speaker.

Edna felt embarrassed that she hadn't realised it was the fire alarm but she wasn't happy about evacuating the hall. 'Where's the fire?' she asked the scout master.

'Not sure. I've looked round the two halls and the kitchen and can't see anything but there is definitely a burning smell coming from somewhere.'

Edna wasn't going to hang around to find out if this was actually a fire or not. Her feeling of responsibility towards her members kicked in. 'Ladies, can you please make your way out to the carpark.' Everyone gathered up their belongings and headed outside. 'I'm sure we won't be too long,' she said to them, hoping that they weren't all going to disappear off home.

Much to Edna's relief, they weren't in the carpark for long and although they had lost part of their evening, the fire brigade arrived quickly and were able to deal with the problem. A couple of the scouts had been having a crafty cigarette and had managed to start a small fire. After this had been put out and the scout master had dealt with the guilty parties, everyone was allowed back into the hall.

Vanda resumed her demonstration despite being slightly pushed for time. She raced through the rest of the exhibits and it wasn't long before the stage was covered in her designs.

As soon as Vanda, finished Freda got to her feet to do the vote of thanks. She often found that she was nominated to do this. Edna refused to as she felt that someone else should have that responsibility, and any of the other committee members rarely offered to do it. 'I wouldn't know what to say,' said Sarah at one of the committee meetings. 'What happens if you think the demonstration is absolute rubbish? How can you say anything nice about it?'

'The trick is to say something like "I can honestly say I've never seen our stage look like this before". That way you don't have to go into specific details,' suggested Freda. After disclosing this information Sarah always found it amusing if Freda made this comment when she did a vote of thanks as she knew exactly what Freda had thought of it.

The vote of thanks on this occasion was relatively easy for Freda as Vanda's demonstration had been good, apart from the fact that no one understood what she was saying and the unexpected interruption. However, her flowers looked incredible, albeit rather rushed.

The audience quickly got their raffle tickets out as Vanda drew the first number.

April couldn't believe her luck as her number was drawn first. She rarely won anything. On the rare occasion she did she invariably ended up with an arrangement she didn't want, but tonight she was getting first pick of all the designs. She chose an incredibly modern design in a handmade container, featuring spray carnations that had been grouped together. There was an amazing twig structure that Vanda had made that set the whole design off.

The rest of the arrangements were claimed by members of the audience and the evening came to a close. Everyone started clearing their chairs and the hall was soon vacated by the members.

April headed to the stage to collect her prize flower arrangement but there was no sign of it. Where it had once stood was now a pile of spray carnations all cut off to a length of about one inch; the counterpart of her raffle ticket was on the stage next to them. 'What's this?' she asked in horror. 'Where's my arrangement? I can't believe that someone has taken it,' she said in disbelief. She glanced over at Vanda who was packing the final items from her demonstration into her bag.

'Do you know where my design is?' she asked her.

'It's here.' Vanda pointed to the pile of flowers.

'Where's the rest of it?'

'I'm afraid that's it. I don't give my containers away and your design incorporated a number of structures I had made that I didn't want to part with.'

'Had I known I was going home with a handful of flower-heads I'd have chosen a different arrangement.' April was furious.

'I don't think the others were much better,' chipped in Lizzy, who had overheard the conversation. 'I saw some of our members walking out with a handful of flowers and they were all moaning.'

'This is hardly going to persuade members to buy raffle tickets if they're disappointed with the prizes. I will definitely be raising this at our next committee meeting.' April felt bitter with the turn of events and headed for home in disgust, cupping the flowers carefully in her hand.

TWENTY-TWO

It took a long time for Sarah to get ready for her blind date. Every outfit she tried on made her look too fat, too old, or too formal. In the end she plumped for a comfortable pair of trousers and a long loose top that helped cover any unwanted bulges, not that she had any to begin with as by most people's standards she was extremely slim.

It had been a while since Sarah had been on a date. She had pretty much given up hoping to meet anyone and had made a life for herself that she was fairly content with. She had obviously had boyfriends over the years, but had never met anyone whom she thought was right for her.

'You're too fussy,' Polly often told her.

'I can't help it if I've got high expectations.'

'Yes, but you'll never meet anyone who's perfect. If they were that perfect you wouldn't like them anyway. We've all got our flaws and baggage.'

Perhaps Polly was right. Sarah had built such a busy life for herself that trying to fit someone in was going to be difficult. She wasn't too sure how much she would be prepared to compromise.

She had one last look in the mirror to check her make-up looked all right and that she hadn't smudged her mascara, took a deep breath, and set off for the garden centre where she'd agreed to meet Colin.

'Where are you going?' enquired Mark.

'Out.'

Mark knew that Polly was up to something. He looked at her. 'Anywhere in particular?'

'Just out.' Polly smiled.

'Come on, tell me where.' Mark was desperate to know what she was up to.

'OK. Sarah's going on a blind date.'

'And?'

'I'm worried about her.'

'So you're going too?' asked Mark in disbelief.

'Not exactly. I know where they're meeting so I'm just going to check all is well.'

'Spy, you mean?'

Polly laughed. 'I suppose so.'

'Where's she meeting him?'

'In the garden centre café.'

Mark pulled a face. 'Does Sarah know you're going to spy on her?'

'Of course not. I'm going to be discreet. She won't even know I'm there.'

Mark sensed that this could be a recipe for disaster. Polly was rarely discreet about anything. 'Do you want me to come too?'

'No. You're far too conspicuous.'

'OK, Agent 008, good luck with your mission.'

'More like Agent Double Over Weight,' said Polly laughing, as she headed to the car.

Sarah arrived at the garden centre a little early. She looked over at the entrance to the café where she had said she would meet Colin. There was no one there. Her stomach churned.

As she was standing waiting she looked everyone up and down, checking them out to see if she could spot him. It wasn't long before a man turned up looking vaguely like the picture she had seen, although it was clear the photo had been taken several years earlier when he had more hair.

'Sarah?' the man enquired.

Sarah nodded. 'I assume you must be Colin.'

'Shall we get a cup of tea?' he asked. Sarah sat down at one of the tables while Colin negotiated the queue and eventually turned up with a tray of drinks.

'Thanks.'

There was an awkward silence. 'So do you come here often?' Sarah joked, trying to break the ice.

'No, it's the first time,' Colin replied.

'Really? You've never come to this garden centre before?'

'I've never been to a garden centre.'

Sarah screwed up her face. 'But I thought you were a gardener?'

'That's right, I am, but I always have plants delivered and I order from catalogues so I don't need to go to a garden centre.'

'But haven't you ever been curious as to what is sold in a garden centre?'

'Not really. Although now I'm here I'm amazed at what they sell. There are some lovely items here.'

Sarah couldn't believe Colin's response and sat quietly wondering what to say next.

Colin took a sip of his tea. 'Where do you work?' he asked, trying to fill the silence.

'In an office in town. I just do clerical work, that sort of thing.'

'You don't sound particularly thrilled about it.'

'No, not really. I work with a strange bunch of people whom I have little in common with. I prefer to do more arty-crafty things rather than pencil pushing.' Sarah was honest with him.

'Why don't you find another job then? One that you'll feel satisfied in?' Colin suggested.

'Easier said than done. Trouble is that when you've got a mortgage and the job market is flat you have to hang on to a job. I can't afford to be out of work or I'll lose everything.'

Colin didn't seem to appreciate Sarah's predicament. 'But if you really hate your job you're better off changing it or you're just wasting your energy.'

'I've found a way around it. I go to work to pay for the things I want to do. After all, surely that's what most people do. If you won the lottery, you'd give up work, wouldn't you?'

'I doubt it. Not that I'm likely to be faced with that problem as I don't do the lottery.' Colin thought for a second. 'What you need to do is make a list of everything that is important to you, then decide what you're going to do with your life.'

Sarah was taken aback by this suggestion. She hadn't imagined that her date would be lecturing her on how to run her life when she'd only just met him. 'I'm happy with my life, thanks,' she replied, as politely as possible.

Sarah was beginning to think that she had little in common with Colin and the conversation was becoming a bit of a strain. She finished her tea without speaking to him. She glanced around and thought she caught a glimpse of Polly. Perhaps that was wishful thinking on her part as it would have given her an excuse to leave.

'Shall we have a wander round?' she asked, trying to take the tension out of the situation. Colin readily agreed as he was clearly keen to see what items were on sale.

Polly had arrived at the garden centre a short time after Sarah. She drove round the carpark a couple of times looking for a parking space and noticed Sarah's car. She managed to find a space just opposite her. She glanced into the garden centre to see if she could spot Sarah. Sarah was sitting in the café with a man who she assumed was Colin. She looked very serious.

Polly waited until some more people were entering the garden centre and she walked in with them in the hope of not being spotted by Sarah. She followed them into the indoor plant section where she decided to loiter, just in case Sarah needed her.

Sarah and Colin walked slowly around the garden centre. Colin was so amazed at the items they sold that he stopped at almost every display, which was beginning to annoy Sarah. They came across a table of highly-decorated pots.

'This looks lovely. I really like this. It would look great in my conservatory.' He held up one of the pots.

'Why don't you buy it? Go on treat yourself,' urged Sarah.

'I'm not sure if Tina would like it.'

Sarah's brain ticked over rapidly. 'Who's Tina?'

'My daughter.' This was the first mention of a daughter and it took Sarah totally by surprise.

'I didn't realise you had a daughter. How old is she?'

'Thirteen. She keeps me under control and gives me her approval on everything I buy.'

'So she tells you what you can and can't buy?'

'Pretty much. There's no way I'd trust myself to buy anything for the house without her approval.'

By now Sarah was well and truly turned off. She hadn't anticipated meeting someone who lectured her on how to run her life and was dictated to by his daughter. It was clear to her that they had nothing in common and she decided to end the date there and then.

She looked at her watch. 'I'm afraid I need to head off,' she lied. 'It's been nice meeting you, Colin.'

'I've really enjoyed this afternoon. Can we keep in touch and perhaps do this again?' asked Colin, clearly more interested than Sarah in having a relationship. She didn't have the heart to say no and agreed, knowing that she had no intention of contacting him again.

She headed out to her car and started to get in when she noticed Polly's car in the row opposite her. She had a look round but couldn't see her. Now she knew that her mind hadn't been playing tricks on her. Polly was definitely somewhere in the garden centre.

As soon as she was sure that Colin had driven off she headed back inside and noticed Polly standing behind one of the stands of seeds, trying to look inconspicuous.

'You can come out now,' Sarah said.

'How did you know I was here?'

'For starters you're parked in the next row to me, plus I

thought I saw you earlier dodging behind the pots of citrus plants.'

'Oh. I wouldn't make a very good spy then, would I?'

'Not really. I doubt MI5 would employ you.'

Polly laughed. 'How did it go?'

'He's a gardener who's never been to a garden centre. His thirteen-year-old daughter tells him what he can and can't buy and he looks about twenty years older than in his photo. Added to which he's on a totally different wave length from me, and seems to think he can tell me what to do.'

'So it went well?'

'Umm. I can do without someone like that in my life.'

'Take it you're not going to see him again.'

'Er, no.'

'Well, back to the drawing board. Fancy having another cuppa and a slice of their speciality apple cake?'

'Sounds like a great plan to me, I'm starving. I didn't have any lunch in case he wanted to buy me lunch or at least a cake. But it didn't even cross his mind.'

'Perhaps he should have asked his daughter what he should do.'

'I'm surprised he didn't bring her along.' Sarah was disappointed. She'd had high hopes for this date. 'Maybe I should have taken Hilda up on the offer of a date with her friend.' She laughed.

'Now that does sound like desperation. Have a piece of cake, you'll feel better then.'

For once, Polly was right.

TWENTY-THREE

The monthly committee meeting had arrived once again. A few of the committee members were missing, most noticeably Barbara.

'Barbara won't be here this evening as she had to have a root canal treatment today and doesn't feel like coming,' Edna informed them, cringing at the thought of dental treatment. 'Polly, would you mind taking the minutes?' she asked.

Polly groaned. 'I suppose not.'

The last time she had taken the minutes she had found herself in a difficult situation at work. Not only had she struggled to decipher her scribble as she was typing the minutes back, somehow she managed to copy a section of them into her boss's board paper. To this day, she is still not sure exactly how it happened but, having spent her lunch-hour typing them up, she saved her work and then moved on to preparing the board papers. She must have still had some text saved on the clipboard on her computer and when she was editing the board paper it somehow found its way into that.

As her boss was doing the final read-through before the papers were issued to the chairman she could tell from his face that something was wrong. It was a mixture of confusion and amusement.

'Polly, can you come here please?' he called from his office.

She got up from her desk and rather sheepishly entered the room. 'Is there a problem?'

'Well, on this page we're discussing the budget process.'

'And?'

'Next minute we're discussing how many pints of milk Barbara needs to buy and that Edna will be making a lemon drizzle cake.'

Polly stared at her boss. She could see laughter in his eyes. 'Oh my God, I'm so sorry,' she said, not sure if it was appropriate to laugh or not. 'I was typing the minutes from my flower club committee meeting at lunch-time. No idea how this ended up in your board paper.'

He burst out laughing. 'Perhaps we should leave this in. It would make our board meeting a lot more interesting.'

Polly never lived this down and was constantly reminded of it, especially during the office Christmas party when people were reminiscing after a few drinks.

She picked up her pen and started to write, determined that she would at least get the minutes right this time. The last thing she wanted was for Julia to find too much to criticise next month.

Edna called the meeting to order. 'Don't worry, Polly, I'll tell you what to write,' she said in quite a patronising way, although she meant this to be a helpful comment as she knew Polly was nervous about taking the minutes.

Everyone was talking about the fire alarm at the last club night.

'That was a bit of a shock,' Freda noted.

'Bet the boys who started the fire got a real rocket,' observed Lizzy, amused by the whole situation and remembering a moment in her teens when she had been caught smoking.

'Wouldn't have wanted to be in their shoes,' said Polly, laughing.

'Apart from the fire alarm, what was the feedback from the evening with regard to Vanda?' Edna asked, curious to know what everyone had thought about the demonstration. Almost before Edna could get the words out April was ranting.

'I was disgusted.'

'Her dem was good, though,' pointed out Edna.

'I'm not complaining about that, apart from the fact that I couldn't understand what she was warbling on about.'

'Yes, she was difficult to understand,' agreed Edna.

'I thought she was talking about her husband until Sarah pointed out that Jasper was actually her dog.' Polly laughed as she remembered the conversation. 'Her designs were stunning, though.'

'Until the raffle,' reminded April. 'She removed so much from each design that all that was left was a few flower-heads. It was pathetic.'

'I agree. It doesn't do much to promote the club. Going forward, Julia, when you book a demonstrator, can you tell them that we don't approve of them removing most of the design of the raffle prize,' instructed Edna.

'If they need to hold on to anything, perhaps they could

say, so that everyone is clear as to what they are winning.' April was determined that no one else would be disappointed the way she had been.

'And if most of the design is being kept, they should give a bunch of flowers to the prize-winner instead,' suggested Sarah.

'That's a good idea, but I'd like to see our members going home with the complete design,' reiterated Edna.

'I understand that she needed her containers, but to remove all the twig structures she'd made was totally unacceptable.' April wouldn't let go of the subject. 'The flowers I won were so short all I could do was float them in a bowl of water. It ruined the evening for me.'

Polly smiled inwardly. Perhaps it was because she had an incredibly full life, but she felt sad for April if an incident like this ruined her evening. By comparison, Polly had found the evening quite amusing.

'While we're on the subject of our last club night, I'd like to point out that if someone puts their name on the cake rota they understand that they must bake the cake. Purchasing one from the supermarket is totally unacceptable,' ranted Edna.

'I think Pamela was busy. She didn't have time to bake but didn't want to let us down.' Julia defended her.

'That might be so, but the rota needs to be taken seriously in future. Our members expect a home-baked cake, not some mass produced rubbish full of E numbers.'

Usually, no one dared argue with Edna, especially not on the subject of cake making since she considered herself to be an expert on all matters pertaining to baking.

'But you bought some cakes the other month,' pointed out Julia.

'No I didn't. I'd never do that,' replied Edna, shocked that Julia should challenge her in this way.

'I think you did,' Polly reminded her. 'You remember the workshop night, there was a problem with the cake you brought with you.' Polly raised her eyebrows.

'What, the pot cake?' asked Lizzy.

Polly glared at her. She knew she should never have mentioned it to her. Edna looked mortified as she glanced at Polly, who mouthed 'sorry' to her. The fact that Lizzy was aware of the incident with the cannabis cake made Edna feel nervous, as she was sure Lizzy would be telling everyone about it.

'They were exceptional circumstances,' defended Edna.

'What do you mean "pot cake"?' Julia asked innocently, just catching up with the conversation.

'Nothing. I wasn't happy with the recipe that I had used so I discarded the cake.' Edna tried to dismiss the subject but realised this wasn't going to be easy.

'All I'm saying is that going forward we should spell it out in our newsletter, so that our members know what is expected of them if they take on the responsibility. Don't you agree?' Edna looked at Sarah and Rose, who were both keeping quiet and not wanting to get involved with the discussion. They burst out laughing.

'It's only a cake,' Rose said, although as soon as the words left her lips she realised that this wasn't something that should have been said out loud, and certainly not within earshot of Edna, who glared at her.

'Well, I totally disagree with you, Rose. We either do this properly or not at all.' Edna looked angry.

'Am I supposed to be minuting all this?' asked Polly, who

by now was scribbling frantically so that she didn't miss out anything.

'Definitely,' replied Edna. 'Put in a note that all cakes served to our members must be home-baked.'

'That stops other people putting their names on the rota. After all, I don't bake, but I'm more than happy to buy something,' admitted Rose.

'Whilst I'm not happy about people purchasing cakes, I suppose it would be acceptable if you bought a home-baked cake – like the ones you buy in the bakery or local farm shops but I don't think we should encourage this,' dictated Edna.

Rose knew that she wasn't going to win this argument with Edna and decided to accept this suggestion.

Edna glanced at the agenda. 'Treasurer's report.' She looked at Hilary.

'Not much has changed since last month.' Hilary reported.

'Hang on a minute,' interrupted April. 'What about the money from the trip to Winchester? I made a profit on that trip plus we raised money for our charity from the raffle.'

'Did we? I don't seem to have that written down.'

'I gave you the money at club night,' insisted April.

'Oh yes. I remember now. I'm sure I wrote it down somewhere,' Hilary replied as her memory slowly started to come back to her one piece at a time. She thumbed through her notebook looking for some record of the transaction. She found some notes scribbled on the back of one of the pages. 'Here it is. We made a £50 profit, plus £30 for our charity. I'll update our records accordingly.'

'If April gave this to you at club night, how come it's not in the figures? And what about the money we raised in the supermarket?' Rose dared to ask. Hilary gave her a filthy look, not appreciating being challenged. 'I'm not accusing anyone of doing anything illegal, I'm just asking the question,' defended Rose.

'That's why we should automate our accounts,' interrupted Polly.

'We're not having *that* conversation again,' snapped Edna, aware that Hilary wasn't privy to the conversation that they'd had about this a couple of months earlier.

'What conversation?' Hilary asked innocently.

'Polly wants you to put the accounts on a spreadsheet,' answered Lizzy.

'A what?'

'A spreadsheet,' reiterated Polly. 'You just enter everything each month, then you print off a report from it for our committee meeting. That way you don't have to work anything out. The program will add it up for you.'

'I can't do that. I don't have a computer. There's nothing wrong with the way I keep the accounts.' Hilary wasn't going to be convinced.

'Can we move on from this?' asked Edna, who was starting to get irritated by the discussion. She always felt like this when she was out of her depth but didn't want to admit it. Change did not come easy to her.

'Can we discuss our website?' asked Lizzy, well aware that this was another controversial subject.

'What about it?' enquired Edna.

'We need to renew it for another two years. Can I have a cheque?'

'Isn't this a complete waste of money? After all, does anyone look at it? I've never seen it,' chipped in Hilary.

'That's probably because you haven't got a computer,' pointed out Rose.

Hilary ignored this fact. 'It just seems an unnecessary expense. What exactly are we paying for?'

'Domain name and web hosting.'

'Web whating?' Hilary was confused.

'We have to pay for the name of our site. Plus, a company hosts it for us. We have to pay for that too,' explained Lizzy.

'I've no idea what you're talking about. I hope you know,' replied Hilary in a patronising way.

'Anyone who is anyone has a website these days. We must have one to promote the club, otherwise we'll never get new members.' Rose defended Lizzy's request.

'You ought to have a look at it, Hilary,' suggested Sarah. 'It's really good. It's got loads of photos of our work on there.'

'I've loaded yours and Polly's latest pictures. They look great,' confirmed Lizzy.

'I had no idea about this.' Hilary was still totally bemused.

'So is the answer yes or no to a cheque?' questioned Lizzy.

Whilst Edna didn't understand much about technology, and was clearly beginning to lose touch with young people, because of this she understood the importance of communicating with them in this way. 'I propose that we continue with the website,' she said, although Lizzy felt quite put out that there was even a suggestion that the committee might not continue with it.

'We ought to set up a blog, and go on other social media sites,' suggested Rose.

'I don't think we will at the moment,' replied Edna, although she had absolutely no idea what Rose was talking about. This was all a foreign language as far as she was concerned.

'I'm happy to do this if you want me to but I'll need regular information for updating,' offered Rose.

'Let's discuss it at our next meeting as time is moving on.' Edna dismissed the suggestion. This would give her time to go away and try to research it to find out what Rose was proposing. 'Who's our demonstrator next month?'

'David Jenkins,' replied Julia.

'Any special requests from him?' Edna didn't want to take any chances following Vanda's long list of demands.

'Nothing other than a cup of tea.'

'That's the sort of person I like,' observed Polly.

'Does he know we're having a tea break and that he can't get in until 7 p.m.?'

'Absolutely. Don't think we'll have any issues this time around,' confirmed Julia, who was not anticipating any problems.

'And I'm on cake duty,' confirmed Polly, much to Edna's relief. 'Not sure what I'm making. Might be an orange chiffon cake.'

Edna was pleased that the next club night should run according to plan and she had no doubt that Polly wouldn't let her down.

'So that's about it for tonight.' Edna ended the meeting.

TWENTY-FOUR

Gillian had just settled down to eat her lunch when the doorbell went. She sighed at the thought of having to leave her steak and kidney pie, which she had been looking forward to eating. Charles had gone out for the morning so she was making the most of having the house to herself.

As she approached her front door she could make out the colour of the police car through the glass panel. Standing on her doorstep were two police officers; a man and a woman. She wondered if perhaps they had discovered something about Robert's death. She trembled, afraid as to why they were there.

'May we come in?'

Gillian didn't answer but instead let the police officers walk into her house. They stood in the hallway while they waited for Gillian to lead the way into her lounge.

'I'm afraid your husband has been rushed to hospital.'

Initially, she didn't take in what they were saying. For a split second she felt relieved that they weren't there to discuss

Robert. 'What do you mean?' she asked. 'He's gone out with some friends.'

'Yes, we know that. He's had a car accident.'

'Is he all right?'

'I'm afraid not. He's in a very bad way. Can we take you to the hospital right now?'

'How ... why ... did he have an accident?' she stuttered.

'That's what we're trying to find out. Was he on any medication?'

'No. Just some herbs my friend gave him.'

'Can you give me the name of the person who prescribed them?'

Gillian was taken aback by the question, not understanding why they wanted to know. 'Well, yes, it was Margery.'

'Braithwaite?' interrupted the police officer.

'Yes.' Gillian was surprised he knew her name. 'How do you know Margery?' The police officer ignored her question.

'Do you know what she gave him?'

'What's Margery got to do with this? I don't understand.'

'If you can just remember what she gave him that might help.'

'I've no idea. I can ask her.' Before the police officer could respond Gillian was on the phone to Margery, telling her what had happened. She handed the phone to the police officer.

'Can you tell me what herbs you gave Mr Matthews?'

'Just some feverfew, camomile, and other herbs like that. It was to treat his headaches,' replied Margery who by now was beginning to worry that she had done something wrong. She deliberately chose to forget to tell the police that she slipped a little cannabis into the mixture.

'Thank you, Mrs Braithwaite. We'll be in touch.' The police officer handed the phone back to Gillian. 'Right now we need to get you to the hospital,' she insisted. 'Can you give me the herbs that he's been taking?'

Gillian went into the kitchen and located the bag of Margery's herbs and the tincture that she had made up for him, and handed them to the police officer. She picked up her handbag and keys, and on the way out of the house collected her jacket which was on the hook in the hallway. As she walked out of her house, she was aware that neighbours were staring over at her and a few curtains had started to twitch across the road from her house.

Her next-door neighbour came out of his house. 'Everything all right Gillian?' he asked.

'It's Charles. He's in hospital,' she replied as she got into the police car.

'I'm so sorry. If there's anything I can do to help, let me know,' shouted her neighbour through the window, but by now Gillian was miles away, thinking about what might or might not have happened, and how come they knew Margery's name.

Margery started shaking as she ended the call with the police officer. She was concerned for Gillian, but also very worried about Charles. Whilst she hated Charles, she hadn't intended him any harm. As far as she was concerned she had just given him some herbs to treat his headaches and calm him down a bit, but doubt was already starting to creep into her head. What if she had been responsible for whatever had happened? Would they find out the actual ingredients of the remedy she had given him?

She wondered what had prompted Gillian to phone her and why the police were interested in the herbs she'd prescribed. She decided to head to the hospital to see how Charles was and try and get some answers.

As soon as Gillian arrived at the hospital she was taken into the relative's room and asked to wait. She could see Margery through the window and she signalled to her. Reluctantly, the police allowed Margery into the room.

'What's going on?' asked Margery.

'I don't know. I'm waiting to speak to the doctor. They just told me to wait here.'

'Why have they got the herbs I gave Charles?' whispered Margery as she noticed a police officer handing the bag of herbs and bottle of tincture over to one of the doctors so that they could be analysed. The doctor looked over at the relatives' room where Gillian was and headed in her direction.

'No idea,' Gillian replied. She had barely finished speaking when a sullen-looking doctor appeared. 'But somehow they knew who you were,' she continued.

Margery felt sick in the pit of her stomach as nerves started to kick in.

The doctor looked at Gillian and Margery. 'Mrs Matthews?' Gillian nodded.

'I'm very sorry to say that your husband has died. We did everything we could.'

Gillian might have hated Charles and thought all kinds of wicked things about him, but the reality of his death hit her hard. She stumbled and was helped to a seat.

'Why did this happen?'

'We're not sure yet. We think he might have blacked out

for some reason. We'll need to carry out a full post-mortem and will let you know our findings in due course.'

'I don't understand. He just went out for the day with friends.' The doctor looked sympathetic but didn't speak. 'Can I see him?' she asked.

'In a minute. One of my nurses will come and get you once we have moved him to the chapel of rest,' replied the doctor as he left the room.

Margery looked pale with shock. 'Gillian, I'm so sorry,' she said, although she was aware that Gillian couldn't hear what she was saying. She was clearly struggling to understand what had happened.

The nurse appeared and offered to take Gillian to see Charles. 'Do you want me to come with you?' asked Margery.

Gillian nodded and took her hand. They both walked into the room to see Charles. He looked so peaceful and, for a second, Gillian felt an overwhelming sense of grief for losing him, especially in this way.

'Let's get you home,' suggested Margery.

Gillian sat at the kitchen table. She hadn't slept all night. Images of Charles's face kept entering her head. She couldn't stop wondering what had happened, why he had blacked out, and how the police knew about Margery.

Her mind went back to the day that she asked Margery to treat Charles. Whilst she hated having bad thoughts about her long-term friend, doubts started to creep into her mind about the treatment Margery had given Charles. She wondered if perhaps Margery had misunderstood her and had taken it upon herself to give Charles something that would make him ill.

TWENTY-FIVE

The traffic was unusually busy on club night and Polly was starting to get annoyed. After the especially heated discussions that had taken place at the last committee meeting, she didn't relish meeting up with some of the committee members. This was made worse by the fact that Sarah wasn't going to be there to offer moral support.

She was already running late. Usually she would head to the meeting straight from work but on this occasion she needed to pop home to pick up the orange chiffon cake that she had made. Being stuck in traffic wasn't helping the situation and she could feel her stress levels rising. The last thing she was in the mood for was a mouthful from Edna when she got to the church hall, as she was supposed to be helping to set up the stage for the demonstrator that evening.

Having inched forward a few feet, Polly noticed a side turning. She decided to turn into it and head across the housing estate, which would take her straight past Margery's house. As she approached the house she noticed several police cars parked outside, the blue lights still flashing. She pulled into the kerb nearby and watched, totally fascinated with what was happening. A police officer headed in her direction. She wound the window down.

'Do you live here?' asked the police officer.

'No.'

'Then would you mind moving on?'

'I know the person who lives here and I just wondered if everything is OK.'

Just as she had finished her sentence she saw Margery leaving the house, accompanied by two police officers. 'Margery,' she called. 'What's happening?'

Margery looked at her. She looked pale and shaken. There was redness round her eyes and she was crying.

'Why are you taking her away?' Polly asked the police officer, who was still standing beside her car.

'I can't answer that question, I'm afraid. I need you to leave now.'

Polly felt obliged to obey so she started up the car engine and slowly moved off down the road. She glanced in her rear view mirror and noticed the police heading out of Margery's house, carrying some of her cannabis plants.

By the time she arrived at the hall, Edna was well into overdrive as she was having to sort the stage out for Polly. She gave Polly a filthy look.

'Sorry I'm late. The traffic was bad,' Polly called out. Edna ignored her. She wasn't in the mood for excuses. 'I came past Margery's house and it looks like she's been arrested.'

Edna stopped what she was doing. Immediately, her annoyance with Polly for being late evaporated. 'What do you mean?'

'Just what I said. The police were carrying out her cannabis plants. Bet she's been done for growing them.'

Edna looked shocked. She had thought about reporting Margery for growing the plants and had decided against it, but now she was worried that Margery would think it was her who had dropped her in it.

It was clear that Edna was upset and shocked by the news, but she needed to pull herself together as her club members were about to arrive and there was still lots to do.

'No plant sale tonight?' asked one of the members when she noticed that Margery wasn't there.

'She couldn't make tonight,' replied Polly.

'That's a shame.'

'Hopefully she'll be here next month.' Polly wasn't sure if they would ever see her again but didn't want to suggest anything to the members until she knew for sure.

'Polly, I've made David a cup of tea and he's getting set up now,' interrupted Edna.

'Thanks. I'll go and see if he needs any more help.' She handed Edna her orange chiffon cake which got a nod of approval.

Edna put it on the table for her, and placed an apple cake that she had made beside it. At least no one would complain about the quality of cakes tonight.

'I think we're ready to start,' advised Polly.

Edna took her place at the front of the hall and greeted all the members before giving out the notices. There was a really good turn out this evening as David was a regular demonstrator at the club and everyone was looking forward to an enjoyable evening.

David began his demonstration. It was extremely

flamboyant, with palm leaves overflowing the container and orchids spilling out from the design. Quite a contrast from Vanda's demonstration last month, where each design seemed to be quite sparse and lacking in flowers. He tended to stick to the more traditional style of flower arranging, but with his own unique style.

Edna was impressed by his amazing designs, but her mind kept going back to the news about Margery. She wondered if she should go round to Margery's in the morning, although the thought crossed her mind that she might still be at the police station.

David was an incredibly fast flower arranger and it wasn't long before he had completed the first half of his demonstration. The stage was already looking fabulous with the selection of flowers. The audience appeared to be totally transfixed by his demonstration, which was always good news for Edna.

The tea break was announced and the members eagerly headed to the cake table, having seen Polly's orange chiffon cake. This was a real favourite with them. In a matter of minutes all the slices had vanished, along with most of Edna's apple cake. Edna inspected the plates and was pleased with the result; quite a contrast from last month's meeting when she had to send Pamela home with most of the uneaten shop-bought cakes.

After the break, David resumed his demonstration, and before long the whole stage was engulfed in his designs. The vote of thanks was incredibly easy for Freda on this occasion, she gushed with enthusiasm as she thanked him for creating such a wonderful display of colours and textures.

The ladies eagerly took out their raffle tickets, although one or two were a little concerned over the size of some of the designs. Several had travelled by bus to the church hall that evening and they weren't sure how they would get the larger arrangements home.

The small designs seemed to be chosen first and it wasn't that surprising, therefore, that the show-stopping pedestal arrangement of palm leaves, sprays of orchids and a selection of wonderfully coloured roses was the last arrangement to be claimed. Whoever won this was definitely taking on a major challenge with getting it home. As luck would have it, Polly's number was called. She was so thrilled to have won this arrangement that the thought didn't cross her mind as to whether or not it would fit in her car.

As soon as the hall was cleared, Polly retrieved the arrangement. It was so large that two people had to dismantle it from the pedestal and hand it to her.

'Are you going to be OK with that?' asked Lizzy, concerned that Polly was disappearing under the weight of it.

'No problem,' replied Polly, excited by her prize, but a little concerned as to how she was going to get it home.

Heads turned as Polly made her way out to the car. Everyone was laughing as they saw a walking flower arrangement with two legs sticking out from the bottom of it.

'Lovely cake, Polly,' called out Edna as she followed her to the car with her cake tin.

Polly put the arrangement on the pavement beside the car and opened the boot. Edna and Polly carefully lifted up the arrangement and tried to slide it into the car but it was far too tall.

'You'll never get it in the car like that, Polly.' Edna stated the obvious. 'Why don't you try putting it on the floor behind the front seats?'

She tried sliding it in carefully, but it kept falling over. By then several pieces of foliage had deposited themselves on the floor of her car. 'I think I'm going to have to take a few pieces out.'

'Good idea.'

Polly took some of the taller flowers and foliage out and was then able to fit it in the back of her car, albeit at a slightly odd angle. 'It should be OK if I drive slowly.'

Edna handed her the empty cake tin.

'What do you think was going on with Margery?' asked Polly, wondering if Edna had any insight as to why the police were there other than for the cannabis.

'I've no idea. I warned her about those damn plants. Why she didn't listen to me is anyone's guess.' Although Edna was worried about Margery she was more concerned that somehow she might find herself in trouble for selling a couple of Margery's plants to club members. She decided not to dwell on it and headed to her car, chuckling as she saw Polly driving off in her overloaded car.

Margery sat in the interview room at the police station. It was stark and unfriendly. She shivered. So much had happened in the last few hours that she was finding it difficult to comprehend her situation.

Two of the police officers who had come to her house entered the room. They could see that Margery was very upset.

'I'm DC Barratt and this is DS Harrow. We need to ask you a few questions with regard to the plants we found at your property and the herbs you have been prescribing.'

Margery nodded. 'What do you want to know?'

'How long have you been prescribing herbs?'

'A number of years. Since my husband passed away. About fifteen years.'

'Are you qualified?'

'No.'

DC Barratt made a note on the paper in front of him.

'You are aware that we recovered a number of cannabis plants from your property earlier today. Can you tell me how long you've been growing them?'

'Since my husband died. He used to take it for his cancer.'

'You are aware that it is illegal to grow it?'

'Suppose so,' replied Margery.

There was a knock on the door. DC Barratt headed outside and returned a few seconds later with a young man.

'Hello, Mrs Braithwaite. I'm Joe Cooper, the duty solicitor.' He sat down beside her. 'Mind if I have a few minutes to talk to Mrs Braithwaite on her own?' he said to the police officers. They left the room as requested but were called back in shortly afterwards.

'Mrs Braithwaite is happy to answer your questions to help with your investigation.'

'Thank you. Who were you supplying the cannabis to?'

'Just a few friends or anyone who needed it for a medical condition.'

'Do you have a distributor?'

Margery looked blankly at him. 'No, should I?'

'I'm just trying to establish if you are growing it to sell or what you are doing with it.'

'I don't charge for it, if that's what you mean. Some people need this drug, so I give it to them.'

'Is that what you gave Charles Matthews?'

Margery didn't reply.

'We are analysing the herbs you gave him so if you did give him this we will find out.'

Margery looked around the room but didn't speak.

'What about Albert Manning, Roslyn Baker and Peter Stuart?' continued DC Barratt.

'Why are you asking me this?' Margery was puzzled.

'These are all people you treated with your herbs?'

'Yes.'

'What did you give them?'

'A variety of herbs. They all had something different.'

'For your information, they all ended up in hospital with various degrees of poisoning. What else were you giving them?'

'You're confusing me. I don't know what you mean. All I did was help them. I never meant to hurt anyone.'

DC Barratt continued scribbling down the information.

'Why did you prescribe herbs for Charles Matthews?'

'Gillian asked me to see him.'

'Is that his wife?'

'Yes.'

'Why did she ask you to see him?'

'He was having headaches and didn't want to see a doctor.'

'Did you treat either of her other husbands?'

'Yes, why?'

'What did you give Charles Matthews?' asked DS Harrow, ignoring her question.

'Just some feverfew for his headaches, and a little camomile to relax him. I might have put in some other herbs. I can't remember.'

'Surely you keep records of what you have been prescribing?' insisted DS Harrow.

Margery looked at her solicitor, tears welling up in her eyes. 'Are you saying that I killed Charles?'

'Did you give him cannabis?' DC Barratt continued with the questioning.

'Maybe I did. You're confusing me.'

'Did he ask you to give him cannabis?'

'No. He left it to me to come up with the mixture of herbs I thought would help him, which is what I did. Did this kill Charles? Is that what you mean? That somehow I'm to blame?'

'No, we're not saying that. We are just concerned that your herbs might have been implicated in his death.'

'Has the post-mortem been carried out?' interrupted Joe Cooper.

'Not yet,' replied DC Barratt.

'In that case you're merely speculating. Are you going to charge my client with anything?'

'Yes. We will be charging her with growing and distributing cannabis.'

Margery was shocked. She could hear Edna's voice in her ear right now and in many ways she wished she had listened to her rather than dismissing what she had to say, but she had never fully realised she might end up in trouble. 'Does that mean they're sending me to jail?' she asked, her voice trembling.

'Not if I have anything to do with it. Just stay calm and let me sort this out,' replied Joe, giving Margery some hope.

Mark had enjoyed a quiet night in watching the television as he always did on a flower club night. A sound he heard outside the front door made him get up. It was a scratching sound, and then some swearing. He opened the door.

Standing on the doorstep was a giant flower arrangement. Polly was so swamped with it that he barely noticed her standing there, trying to balance it in one hand and unlock the door with the other.

Mark burst out laughing. 'Now I've seen everything.' He took the flowers from Polly and she retrieved her house keys that she had managed to drop on the ground.

He placed the arrangement down on the dining-room table which was totally enveloped by it.

'Isn't it fabulous?' asked Polly as she inspected it. There were several gaps where she had removed plant material so she decided to try and recreate the design by filling these gaps. Other pieces had fallen out on the journey home as, despite attempting to drive slowly, sadly she'd had an occasion where she had to brake quite suddenly and more pieces ended up on the floor.

'Lovely,' he replied, feeling slightly overwhelmed by the size of the design. 'Had a good evening then?'

'It was great, but you'll never guess what?'

Mark looked at her. He was slightly intrigued. Polly's eyes were lit up with excitement so she was obviously in possession of some scandal.

'Put the kettle on and I'll tell you all about it.'

TWENTY-SIX

'Murder? What do you mean?' asked Polly.

'Margery has been charged with murder.' Lizzy replied, a hint of excitement in her voice.

'I thought she'd been arrested for growing cannabis.'

'That's the least of her worries.'

'Who's she supposed to have killed?'

'Gillian's husband, Charles.'

'How did she do it?' Polly was curious.

'I gather he was poisoned.'

The very mention of poison got Polly's brain working overtime.

'It's not quite as it seems.' Edna tried to bring reason into the conversation. 'And she hasn't been charged with murder.'

'Turns out that some of her herbal concoctions are lethal.' Lizzy ignored her.

'I wonder if she killed Henry and Robert too.' Polly was convinced there was more to this story.

'Now that's speculating,' Edna replied. 'As I said, she hasn't actually been charged with murder.'

'Yes, but digitalis can cause heart attacks.'

'And valerian and hops can cause sleepiness.' Lizzy and Polly were carried away with speculation.

'If you'll both let me get a word in I'll tell you what's happened.' Edna looked sternly at both of them. 'Charles went to see Margery for headaches.'

'Is Gillian implicated?' interrupted Polly.

'I gather they did take her in for questioning as well as she was the person who got Charles to see Margery,' Edna continued, trying to bring the conversation back to the subject in hand.

'See, I knew she was a murderer.'

'Will you stop interrupting and calling her a murderer.' Edna glared at Polly. 'Now what was I going to say? Oh yes, Gillian's been released with no charge.'

'So, she's got away with it?'

'I don't think she had anything to do with it,' insisted Edna.

'Strange though. I wonder if she referred her other husbands to Margery too.'

'Who knows. Henry and Robert were both cremated anyway.'

'What do you mean, Robert was cremated? I didn't think they'd found his body.' Lizzy wasn't up to date with the story.

'They found him. Turns out he was on the ship all the time.'

Lizzy and Polly looked shocked. 'What d'you mean, on the ship all the time?'

'It would appear he fell in between some of the machinery and that's where he's been ever since,' replied Edna, pleased that she was in possession of this information.

There was a stunned silence. 'You mean to tell me he's been there all the time?' reiterated Polly, totally baffled by what Edna had said.

'Yes,' replied Edna.

'And no one found him until now?' Polly continued the questioning.

'Absolutely. It doesn't bear thinking about.'

'I can't believe that. Surely someone would have found him.'

'Or smelled him,' chipped in Lizzy.

'Thank you, Lizzy. I know this is a shock, but the fact is that I doubt Gillian or Margery had anything to do with his death.'

'So why have they arrested Margery then? Do they think she's implicated in some way in Charles's death?' questioned Sarah.

'Turns out that a few people who saw her became ill and a doctor at the hospital asked the police to pay her a visit. There they not only discovered all her cannabis plants they discovered somewhat dodgy herbs too,' Edna informed them.

'So, was she mixing lethal potions or something?' asked Barbara, who was intrigued by the conversation.

'I don't think she deliberately set out to hurt anyone. More like she's just ignorant. I don't think she was ever registered with any governing body – that was part of the problem,' continued Edna.

'When will we know what happened?' Polly was desperate to get the full story.

'The results of the post-mortem haven't come through yet as far as I'm aware. Gillian said she'd call me as soon as she hears anything. But I'm pretty certain Margery hasn't been charged with murder or anything like that. They don't know if she was implicated in Charles's death as yet.'

'Well, it's all a bit odd if you ask me.'

Not that anyone was asking Lizzy, so Edna ignored her comment. 'When I hear anything I'll let you know. Anyway, ladies, can we get back to the subject in hand; namely the fish and chip supper next month.'

'Last year it was a real success. I think everyone enjoyed themselves. Polly, are you happy to organise it again?' Polly was beaming with pride that she had made such a success of the evening. She didn't really want to commit herself to much at the moment while she tried to come up with ideas for the forthcoming competition, but before she realised it, she was agreeing to take this on again.

'Well done, Polly,' chipped in Freda, who was pleased that she didn't have to do it.

Polly was left wondering why she had been so gullible.

TWENTY-SEVEN

J oe had managed to get Margery bail and she was allowed home whilst they awaited the results of the post-mortem. She didn't particularly want to be in her house as it seemed quite empty now that the police had removed a large number of her beloved plants. Every room felt as though it had been invaded and it no longer felt like a home.

She sat down on the chair in the conservatory and started to cry. How she wished that Duncan was still with her, although had he been alive perhaps she wouldn't have got into such trouble. The phone interrupted her thoughts. It was Gillian.

'Are you all right, dear?' she asked, genuinely concerned.

'I think so.'

'What's happening? Have they charged you with anything?'

'Yes. Growing and distributing cannabis. They're waiting for the results of Charles's post-mortem and said they would let me know if there are any other charges. They said I might be charged with manslaughter.' Margery was distraught. 'I can't believe anyone would accuse me of something so terrible.'

There was a long pause while Gillian tried to think of something to say. 'I don't believe you had anything to do with his death, Margery,' she said, trying to reassure her.

'As far as I'm concerned, all I did was give him a few herbs. I never meant any harm.' Margery started to cry again. 'They asked me so many questions. I got confused and didn't know what to say.'

'But you had a solicitor?'

'Yes. A nice young man called Joe. He told me that he will sort all this out for me so I don't have to go to jail. This is all such a dreadful mess.'

'I'm sure the post-mortem will prove that you had nothing to do with Charles's death.'

'What about the others?'

'What others?'

'They said I'd poisoned other people who had come to me for remedies. Apparently several had ended up in hospital.'

'Why on earth would they say this?' Gillian was fully aware of the accusations as the police had questioned her at some length over Margery's ability to prescribe herbs, but she didn't want to worry Margery.

'The police said that my herbs had made people ill and that it was all my fault.'

'How ridiculous is that?'

'I just remember Duncan telling me to be careful. I know that sometimes I get a bit muddled, but I never wanted to hurt anyone.'

'I know you didn't. Try not to worry about it.' Gillian had been a bit concerned about Margery's ability to prescribe herbs but had never raised the subject with her.

No sooner had Gillian put the phone down than it rang again.

'Hello, Mrs Matthews, this is the coroner's office.'

Gillian took a deep breath and waited to hear the verdict.

'We believe your husband suffered from a condition called cardiac syncope. This is caused by a problem that affects the regulation of blood pressure. It would have caused a momentary blackout.'

Gillian was shocked. She had never heard of this. 'So it was just a terrible accident?'

'Yes. It was just very unfortunate that your husband was driving at the time.'

'What about the herbs he'd been taking?'

'We analysed them and can't say that they would have been responsible for this. They would have caused him to be sleepy, but wouldn't have caused a blackout.'

'He'd been suffering from headaches. Do you think these might have had something to do with it?'

'Possibly. Persistent headaches can indicate that something is wrong.' The coroner didn't give any more details. 'I've got his death certificate ready for your collection.'

Gillian thanked him and immediately phoned Margery with the news.

Margery was still sitting in her empty conservatory when Gillian phoned to tell her the verdict. She was overcome with relief that she hadn't been found guilty of having anything directly to do with Charles's death.

However, her future still hung in the balance. She knew that Joe was fighting on her behalf to prevent her from going to prison, and that she would never again be allowed to prescribe any herbs. Not that this was a problem for her as, after the past events, her desire to do this had waned. But growing and prescribing herbs had become such a large part of her life since Duncan's death that she had no idea how she would fill her life without it. She sat and pondered her future.

Polly awoke at the sound of the dawn chorus. Not that it took much to wake her as she was sleeping so lightly these days. What with thoughts about Gillian and Margery going through her mind, and images of her latest design filling her head, she was finding it difficult to switch off.

She lay still, or at least as still as she was able to. Mark was fast asleep beside her so she carefully got out of bed, trying not to disturb him. She knew it would be difficult to get back to sleep so she headed downstairs to the kitchen and made herself a cup of tea. She wandered into the living-room where she had set up her latest creation. For now it was a collection of drainpipes, vases and anything else she could lay her hands on while she tried to get the design firmly in her mind. At which point she would get Stephen involved and give him the unenviable task of trying to translate the image she had in her head into something stunning in reality.

She crept back to the bedroom and tried to get into bed without waking Mark but he was already wide-awake, wondering where she had gone.

'Can't sleep?'

'No. I keep thinking about the show.'

'It's not for another month. You can't afford to have sleepless nights now.'

'I can't help it. I'm worrying about my arrangement.'

Mark sighed. 'What's there to worry about? I'm sure it'll be great.'

'Yes, but I have doubts.'

'Can't you have these doubts during the day and not the middle of the night?' he reasoned.

Mark was right. What was the point in worrying now? But Polly knew that she was always stressed for months before a big show and these stresses seemed to rear their ugly heads in the quiet hours of the night.

'I know I get stressed, but also I want to know if Amy is competing as I really don't want to face her again. What happens if my stand collapses again, what if…?'

'No more "what ifs". After all, you came first in the last big show. Isn't that enough? If it's going to stress you so much, don't do it.'

'You know I have to do it. I just can't stop entering these shows, even though I know how ill they're going to make me. I don't want people to think I'm a one-hit wonder. I've got to prove it to myself and others that I can arrange flowers.'

'You don't have to prove yourself to anyone. We all know you can arrange flowers extremely well. This is supposed to be a fun hobby, not something that stresses you.'

Polly smiled. 'I know what you're going to say; after all this is just a bunch of flowers.'

'Exactly. Now go back to sleep.'

 Matador

For exclusive discounts on Matador titles,
sign up to our occasional newsletter at
troubador.co.uk/bookshop